WATERCOLOR MEMORIES

a Forbidden Island novel by

LIANNE SIMON

Faie Miss Press

Watercolor Memories
Lianne Simon
ISBN 978-0-9851482-8-7
Copyright © 2020 by Lianne Simon
All rights reserved

Published by Faie Miss Press
Springfield, Tennessee
www.faiemiss.com
www.liannesimon.com
liannesimon@yahoo.com

PUBLISHER'S NOTES

This is a work of fiction. Names, characters, places and incidents either are the product of the author's imagination or are used fictitiously, and any resemblance to actual persons, living or dead, business establishments, events, or locales is entirely coincidental.

The publisher does not have any control over and does not assume any responsibility for author or third-party websites or their content.

Individuals depicted in the images are models and used for illustrative purposes only.

Set in Yana and Bridone Light

Printed in the United States of America

WATERCOLOR MEMORIES

Chapter One

My breasts chafe raw beneath the binder, crying for release. I rub a weary arm across my forehead, then down the front of my jersey in a futile attempt to ease the pain.

Ben slaps my back. My other teammates do as well. Finally, Dylan throws an arm around my shoulder and pulls me close. "Awesome shot," he says.

Dylan—a tremor runs through my exhausted muscles in answer to his touch. "Yeah. Guess so."

"No. Seriously, dude. You won us the match."

I glance up to see if he's joking, but his brown eyes say only that he knows I'll never admit my love for him. Which I won't. 'Cause I'm not into boys.

His smile twitches up on one side before he wanders away. I roll my eyes in frustration. Dylan protects me from bullies. I get that. Really. But sometimes I wish he'd back off a little.

This pretty girl steps out of the crowd and parks herself in front of me. She's my height. Has my pale blonde hair. And my father's Russian eyes.

Papa's abuse—two years distant now—still terrifies me. Muscles tense for flight. Tears gather. Yet part of me yearns to hold the girl close. Forever. Even if she can't be my sister.

She seems content to stare.

I stop and rub at my aching chest again. "Hey. Name's Anatoli." Well, Anya, really.

She grasps my trembling hand in hers. Doesn't shake it. Doesn't let go. I hope she won't. Ever. 'Cause I need her close by. Whoever she is.

Steel blue eyes search mine with eagerness. "I'm Pasha," she says. "My birth name was Praskovya Kyrillovna Gilyova."

"Pashenka?" That tender name escapes my lips before I can think to suppress it. I don't care, though. I search the girl's face more intently. Yeah. She could be the twin I haven't seen in more than five years.

Her face glows with victory. The girl leans close and whispers, "And that would make you?"

My chest tightens. Yeah. Me. "Anna Kyrillovna Gilyova. Anya. Your sister." Playing soccer as a boy.

A single tear scurries down the girl's face. She hugs me tight before pressing something hard into my palm. "I love you, Annushka," she says. After leaving a warm kiss on my cheek, she turns and walks away.

Deafness thunders between my ears. Muscles refuse to do more than twitch. Too late, I reach a hand after her. "Pasha? Don't leave!" The girl's already lost in the crowd, though. Gone. Probably forever this time. Why didn't she stay?

Exhausted, I flop down on the ground and examine my sister's gift. On my palm lies a silver heart on a chain, almost hot enough to burn my skin. A pastel blue St. Andrew's cross glows somewhere deep within the metal. As I watch, the heat fades to a comfortable warmth and the light dims.

Faded memories of a Christmas long ago drift past. We were poor then, but Mamochka—my dear mother—gave me her charm and Pasha her set of matryoshka dolls. My sister's nesting dolls—the one toy that remains from our broken childhood—sits on a shelf next to my school books, in my bedroom at my foster parents' house.

Why return the necklace today? And what caused the metal to glow? Not since I was a toddler have I witnessed that. Back then, I imagined it fairy magic. My pulse throbs in my temples as I clasp the chain around my neck and drop the heart beneath my jersey.

A shadow passes across the noonday sun. I look up into the face of my bestie.

Brit nods toward the soccer field. "You ever gonna come out to Dylan?"

Tell the captain that one of his best players is intersex—and mostly female? No way. So I kiss my bestie instead.

Brit finds it amusing that people think I'm her boyfriend. Not that she's got any reason to want me, she bein' a Junior, with her own car and all. The girl throws me an awesome smile, though. "You ready?"

"Yeah."

She grins like we're keeping the biggest secret in the galaxy. Then we walk off hand-in-hand to her car. As we drive out of the parking lot, I pull off my knit beanie and shake my hair free. Then I text my foster mother.

PKGilyova >> FosterOfTwo — We won!
    Lunch date with Brit.
    Plus an overnighter.

Is it my fault Mom assumes I'm playing on a girls' team?

FosterOfTwo >> PKGilyova — Great! Have fun.

Yeah. The Randalls do the foster thing well. Always positive with me and Heather. They encourage us in all the girly stuff, too, though I'm not much good at it any longer. Anyhow, my hanging out with Miss Bridgitte P. Andrews should make them happy. My bestie's a total femme, even though she doesn't much like her name.

We pull into the driveway at the Andrews' old brick house. Brit's mom is outside, working in her garden. She pulls off her gloves and walks toward us as we coast to a stop beside the back porch. The woman hugs me as soon as I step out of the car. "Good to see you again, Anya."

"Thanks."

Mrs. Andrews is a Christian. Conservative as all get out. She's also a single mom who loves her gay daughter and welcomes into her home a stray intersex kid whose gender isn't entirely clear.

I breathe deep of freedom—and a family that loves me. They'd let me stay forever, but the court will never allow it. Too poor. Too small a house. Whatever other excuses they can find.

The woman hugs Brit before handing her daughter the gloves. "You mind? I'll start lunch."

"No, Ma. You go right ahead. We'll finish up out here."

My bestie grins at me. As usual, one of the neighborhood cats is rubbing against my leg. Not sure why animals like me, but I stoop to pet him before walking to the house to get another set of gloves.

With the cat supervising us, I help my bestie in the garden—till sweat plasters the hair to my face, and burns my eyes. Then I walk into the house and up the stairway.

I find a dress in the hallway closet—a cotton floral print, with a Peter Pan collar and a full skirt. The colors have faded, but I don't care. Fifties farm girl suits me just fine. I slip into the bathroom to bathe and get dressed.

My uniform top's baggy—to hide my figure. Under my jersey's a snug T-shirt. I take both of those off and toss them to the floor.

I'm growing taller and thinner—almost fast enough to watch it happening in the mirror. Strange for a fifteen-year-old girl, but I refuse to see a doctor. My boobs are getting smaller as well, but my binder's still too tight. Like maybe my rib cage is expanding. I roll the binder tenderly up past my itching breasts, wriggle it off over my shoulders, and set it on the counter by the sink.

The soccer shorts fit loosely as well, with an elastic waist. I stuff them—along with my uniform top—into my gym bag. I'll wash them and leave them here.

My packer—that penis-shaped funnel that lets me stand when I pee—is wearing out. Not that it gets much use. It's silicone, but one of the cheaper models. I don't need the thing while playing soccer, but it gives me a weird sort of confidence on the field—like I really am one of the guys. So—hey—why not? I drop it into the sink, along with the harness that keeps it in place.

I step into the shower and twist the knob. Under the steaming torrent of water, my tension melts away. I'm almost sixteen. I can survive another two years. At eighteen, I age out of the foster care system and can be whoever I want.

Except that I want to be Anya again, and my body isn't going back to what it was. Groaning, I lean back against the tiles, close my eyes, and let the water soothe my aching breasts.

Mamochka insisted I'd be happier with a new family—away from Papa. Our father abused Pasha the most, though. So I gave my sister my little heart and a princess T-shirt. So she could be Anya. I played with her nesting dolls instead. We fooled Papa. He gave Pasha to the adoption lady.

My mother screamed at him when she got home, then held me tight and wept for her little Annushka. After that, Papa had only me and Mamochka to hit.

Pasha left five years ago. Mamochka's been gone for two. Both seem like forever. But today, my sister returns my heart. Why now? And why not stay?

Pasha. The soap falls from my hand. My height? My hair? No. My identical twin sister's at least six inches shorter than me now. She still has pale blonde hair and blue eyes. Whatever's happening to me hasn't touched her. Not yet.

I turn off the water, towel myself dry, and step out of the shower. Leaning close to the mirror, I run fingers through my hair. A year ago my curls were a pale blonde. Now my roots are somewhere between strawberry and ginger. What is my body doing?

I baby powder the more sensitive areas of my breasts before finding a bra in my drawer. Undies follow that. Then a slip and a dress. I blow dry my hair and do my makeup. When I finally look like a girl again, I walk down the hallway to our work room.

The Andrews buy and sell vintage clothing. The nicer stuff sells fast. The rest they give away or auction off. No deliveries today, though, so I work on minor repairs to a few dresses—mostly stitching up loose seams and replacing missing buttons.

"Girls!" Mrs. Andrews' voice echoes up the stairwell. Lunch is ready.

We hold hands while Brit's mother asks her God to bless our food. A tear escapes before I can blink it away. She reminds me so much of my mother. Is it wrong to still want Mamochka back?

After we eat, Brit and I clear away the dishes, rinse them, and stack them all in the dishwasher. By the time we're finished, Mrs. Andrews has the table clean and her Bible out.

She's Baptist. Mamochka took me with her every Saturday to a Russian Orthodox church. To worship the same God that allowed Papa to beat her. Yet Mamochka's Savior granted us a peace there we found nowhere else.

My father didn't hit us in church, never showed his face in our sanctuary. But I carry his bruises with me still. For Papa I was never pretty enough. Never feminine enough. Mamochka loved me just the same. So does Brit's mom.

Mrs. Andrews slides her fingers over mine and smiles encouragement. "I'm still praying that we can adopt you, sweetheart."

She reads from Isaiah Chapter 54—God's promise to bless the barren woman with more children than the married one—a barren woman who might well have been intersex. After she's done, she prays for me and for Brit.

I remain quiet long after Mrs. Andrews finishes. A massive storm gathers on the far horizon of my soul. Not long before the rain washes away my life. What's left of it, anyhow. My hand wanders up to the heart at my throat—Mamochka's precious gift to her daughter. Anya. The girl I used to be. The air grows thick and hot around me. I haven't been completely female for nearly a year. Not since my body started changing.

All the emotional turmoil of my past rolls over me—a tsunami of despair. I hop up out of my seat and push the memories away. "I should go," I say. Unable to stop the tears, I rush up the stairway to Brit's room to change into my own clothes. Back to the reality of my foster family.

In my bestie's room I strip down to my undies and stand facing the mirror. If I had any guts, I'd tell the Randalls what's going on. They'd freak at what's between my legs, though, and I'd get sent off to another placement. Like I was suddenly a threat to my foster sister.

Brit pokes her head through the doorway and eyes me with concern. "You all right?"

Part of me wants to run away. Leave my insanity behind, forever abandoned in childhood dreams. My body's not gonna change back to what it was. A tear runs down my cheek. Another follows. Brit slides her arms around my waist and pulls me close. I press my face against her shoulder and weep.

Minutes pass before my bestie speaks again. "You got decent grades, didn't you?"

My shoulders climb up in a careless shrug. "Yeah."

"Why are you so down, then?"

I search Brit's eyes and find only tender concern there. "Sorry," I say and kiss her cheek. Yeah, I'm gonna miss the girl. Words fail me, though. So I chew on my lip while my bestie waits.

In the end, I let go of hope. Of the last faint light of my dream of having a life. "They say I have to see an endocrinologist and a gyne-cologist. Maybe a gender specialist."

"They who?"

"I don't know. The court. My case worker. My foster parents."

"Why can't you just be who you are?"

"They think I might have an intersex condition. Or be taking drugs of some kind."

"So you're tall and have muscles. Who cares? You're still a girl. And a pretty one."

"Am I? With what's between my legs?" She's seen me naked. She knows.

My bestie rolls her eyes. "You've got a large clitoris. So what? It ain't a penis. And you don't have any lumps down there."

"In guys with a 5-alpha reductase deficiency, the genitals look female at birth, but get more masculine at puberty. The testes descend. They can father children."

"Guys with 5-alpha don't menstruate."

"I don't either."

"But you used to."

True. I did. Till about six months ago. But that wasn't my point. "I want to be Anya again, okay? Petite and feminine. I don't like what's happening to my body. Or my gender."

My bestie's sad eyes consider me for a moment before she draws me close again. "Look, Annushka, most of the girls at school are jealous of your looks. You're awesome pretty. All right?"

"Yeah. I guess it has to be." The tears have stopped, but my nose is running. I slip out of Brit's arms, make my way to the bathroom, and wash my face.

"Up for modeling some clothes?" my bestie asks.

When I nod and start putting on makeup, Brit grins and rushes to the closet where she keeps her beloved photography gadgets.

An image of a girl wearing a sixties outfit sells a vintage gown way faster than a picture of that same old dress on a hanger. Brit's awesome with a camera. Me—I'm petite. Well, I used to be. Petite's bad for the runway, but good for modeling vintage clothes.

Pick an outfit, quick change, check my hair and makeup, smile for the camera—I spend the next three hours in an endless cycle of poses and flashing lights. After Brit retakes photos of four of the gowns, we're finished. The dark clouds have dissipated. For now.

Brit tugs at the lace trim on the bust of the dress I'm wearing. "Ma says you can keep this one. An early birthday gift. Her thanks for all the help you've been."

Satin and tulle with velvet trim and a crinoline petticoat—I run a hand down over the full skirt. When the dress arrived in a bulk ship-ment of clothes, it was missing buttons and coming apart in places. Like me. We all spent a lot of love and energy restoring the gown.

My eyes drift across the room to the racks of dresses. In the past few months my fondness for vintage styles has grown. Of all the lovely gowns that have passed through this room, the one I'm wearing is my favorite—an awesome combination of delicate fabrics and colors.

Fancy enough for a party. But too much for wandering around an old house. "That's sweet, Brit. Not like I'd ever wear it, though."

Mischief spreads across the girl's face. "Maybe Dylan would take you to the prom."

"Yeah. Like that's gonna happen." I hug my bestie, return the gown to one of the racks, and change into my old farm girl dress again. Another hour drifts past as Brit and I post the best photos to their online shop.

At six, Mrs. Andrews calls us downstairs for supper. I've just finished setting the table when the doorbell rings. Brit's mashing potatoes. Her mother's cutting up a melon. "I'll get it," I say and walk down the hallway to the back porch.

Dylan—heat flashes through me at his unexpected presence. My chest tightens, but I answer the door anyhow. The boy's lips form a small circle and then curve up into a smile. "You must be the girl who models clothes for the Andrews. Who plays soccer as Anatoli and basketball as Pasha."

I glance behind me to find my bestie peeking around the corner. She nods encouragement. I bob my head at Dylan, pull the door open farther, and step out of the way so he can come in.

The boy's face shines with tender affection. I imagine so anyhow, though he's smiled at me that way for months. I can be kinda dense. Dylan's been in love with Anatoli since the day they met.

I back up as the boy draws closer. A soft snicker drifts down the hallway from Brit's general direction. Dylan rests his hands against the wall, one on either side of me. "I came to see if you'd go to the park with me tomorrow afternoon."

My chest pounds crazy as the seconds tick by. Will he be angry if I say no? Will he hurt me if I go with him? Dylan's never been mean to me. Ever. I've spent hours on the back of his motorcycle, with my arms tight around his waist. The boy's safe.

Pasha, he said. So he knows my legal name. And that I live with the Randall family. I draw in a deep breath, hoping to calm myself. "Is three okay? I'll be home by then. My foster home."

"Sure." He turns to leave, but pauses in the doorway. "I love you, Anatoli."

Anatoli. Not Pasha. I stand there in silence as he walks back out to his motorcycle and drives away. So many questions. He's a friend, but what will he do when I tell him I'm not into boys? I press both hands to my head. I'm gonna have a migraine.

Brit tugs on my arm. "Come on. Supper's getting cold." I follow her to the kitchen and sit at the table, but my mind remains lost in some other dimension. I've got a crush on a boy. Me. Anya.

Mrs. Andrews made Broccoli Chicken Divan—my favorite. One advantage of having a body that keeps getting taller and thinner is that I can eat whatever I want without gaining weight. Too bad I'm not hungry.

All during the meal Brit keeps smiling at me. My face burns. Mrs. Andrews glances at both of us, but doesn't say anything.

After I load the dishwasher, I walk back upstairs. Terror lurks in the shadows. The ghostly image of a tall young woman startles me, but it's only my reflection in the hallway mirror. Memories of Papa sigh in the night. "He'll find you," they whisper. "He'll hurt you again."

"No." I say it aloud. Some night, I'll stand right here, all dressed up like a princess. Mamochka will be proud of her daughter.

I make my way to the back room. With a needle and thread in hand, I settle into the old wicker couch. Two hours later I'm finished stitching. No more clothes in need of repair. I pull out the watercolor I'm doing for Brit, but there's not enough time to work on it. So I put it back, walk downstairs, and step outside.

A full moon rises in the east, its face silhouetting the trees. Somewhere close by, a dog barks. A breeze plays an angel's aria on the wind chimes. What will become of me tomorrow? How many more nights before it all ends, and the curtain drops on the play?

Eventually, Brit opens the door. "Come on to bed," she whispers. I follow the girl to her room and change clothes. I find a nightgown in my drawer—a vintage one with layers of nylon and chiffon. A couple of small tears in the fabric make it a reject. It's comfy soft, but hides very little. Brit's seen me naked, though, so the sheerness of the négligée doesn't matter. I crawl into the squeaky bed, snuggle close to Brit, and shut my eyes.

Mrs. Andrews accepts her daughter's sexual orientation. But in this house, Brit and I are sisters. Not that the girl would ever want me as a lover. Anyhow, I'm like crazy tired, okay?

Chapter Two

A soft tapping drags me out of a hopeless nightmare. My eyes flutter open in the dim light. Brit lies behind me, arms around my waist, her face pressed into my hair. The girl's breath against my neck remains the slow and steady rhythm of sleep.

Mrs. Andrews eases the door open, pads across the room, and sits on the edge of the mattress in front of me. I'm in bed with her daughter, yet she trusts us to behave. I will never disappoint her. Ever.

She leans down and brushes the hair away from my eyes. "We have a guest. Get dressed and come to the kitchen. All right, girls?"

"Yes, Mamochka." My eyes do a slow blink. I've never called the woman that before. But—yeah—I want her to be my mom. Bad.

Brit sits up. "All right, Ma," she says.

Mrs. Andrews smiles, kisses both of us on the cheek, and then leaves. A glance at the clock shows it's twenty after six. I pull the drapes open. In the driveway sits a police cruiser, its blue lights flashing. A black Escalade's parked on the street.

Crazed memories of my mother's death wash over me. The cops swarming around us. Me kicking and biting and screaming as an officer drags me away from Mamochka's body. I jump when someone touches me. It's only Brit, though. "Better hurry," she says.

The hallway's empty, so I rush to my closet and grab my embroidered peasant blouse and bellbottom jeans. Then I run back to the bedroom and finish getting dressed. Chest pounding, I follow my bestie downstairs to the kitchen. A blond-haired man in a dark blue jacket sits at the table, holding a coffee cup with both hands. Down his sleeve runs US MARSHAL. I'm screwed.

Tender joy spreads across the dude's face as I approach, yet he says nothing. Plates full of bacon, eggs, and toast already occupy the table, so I take my usual seat. Mrs. Andrews glances at our visitor and gives me another Mamochka smile before bowing her head. "Lord, please bless this food. Help it to nourish our bodies. Please watch over our conversation. In Jesus' name."

US marshal inside. Cop car outside. Black SUV. Maybe the nice officer just wants to chat. Right. I take a bite of toast and study our visitor again. The dude's too happy for a cop. Unless he thinks Brit and I are criminal masterminds, and he's just captured us.

No. Not Brit. The dude ain't lookin' at my bestie. Just me. Like he's found his long-lost kid. Yeah. His daughter. Eyes don't lie, you know. The guy wouldn't love some random intersex juvenile delinquent that much. My hand wanders up to the heart at my throat. The stranger nods—just a slight tilting of his head. Too late now. Yeah, thanks, Pasha.

After we finish breakfast, I rinse the plates and glasses and silverware and find room for them in the dishwasher. Afterwards, I return to the table. Like they'd let me leave now.

The cuckoo clock in the hallway squawks seven. The bird's not used to having the house overrun by cops.

A US passport lies on top of a manila folder in front of our guest. Mrs. Andrews picks it up and hands it to me. "Is this yours, sweetheart?" The doubt in her eyes—that I might have lied to her—rips at my soul.

I take the passport from her. Anna Ilyinichna Koshkina, it reads. With my birth date and what might as well be my photo from a year ago. Not me, though. My sister. "No, ma'am." I shake my head and hand the passport to the man who has got to be Pasha's adoptive father.

My sister ran away. But how long ago? And why?

The man sighs in frustration. "My name is Ilya Koshkin. I'm your— I'm Anya's father."

I put on my most winsome smile and nod. "I'm Anya. But not your daughter. Sorry."

Sad eyes hold mine for a moment before the guy speaks again. "Your mother gave you that necklace when you were seven."

"Yeah. She did. So?" If I win this debate—if I convince this man that I'm not Pasha—then I get to stay here and die. Or get put into some detention center. If I lose, I go with this dude and find out why my sister left home. Probably not good either way.

Pasha set this in motion, though. Do I trust her? Yeah. 'Cause we protect each other. No matter what. Pretending to be Pasha won't work, though. 'Cause I don't have my sister's memories.

The man opens his manila folder and sets aside a number of photos and papers. He slides a newspaper clipping across the table. "My daughter went missing a year ago." Local girl disappears. Last seen near Beachwood Place Mall. Reward offered for information.

Next, the guy passes across a photo of me wearing a halter top —one from the online shop, no doubt—and a similar picture of my sister. The faces look identical, at least from that angle. My hair's a little shorter, but that's about the only difference. Both images have lines and measurements, like from some facial recognition thing.

"The trail led here," he says, his chin tipping up a bit. Anger shines from the dude's eyes now. No. He ain't mad. Just eager to crush me in this debate. To prove beyond any doubt that I'm his daughter.

The guy sets a handful of legal papers on top of the photos. "Anya's original birth certificate," he says. A fingertip underlines the name—Anna Kyrillovna Gilyova. Yeah. Me. Commonwealth of Pennsylvania. Erie County. My birth date. My biological parents.

Papa. Sitting in his prison cell, does my father think about the family he destroyed? I glance up at Mrs. Andrews and nod. "This one's me, alright. But it doesn't make me his daughter."

The next paper's a certificate of adoption. The new name reads Anna Ilyinichna Koshkina—the old one Anna Kyrillovna Gilyova, of course. Kinda hard to deny that they legit adopted me and changed my name.

A second sheet of paper clings to the first. Voluntary Termination of Parental Rights. Mamochka gave me up for adoption. Me. Her little Annushka. To save me from Papa.

My diaphragm spasms. The storm crashes over me. "Mamochka! Ya skuchayu po tebe!" Someone wails like a toddler in pain. Tears cascade down my cheeks. I jump up out of my chair, and flee the room.

Behind me, Mrs. Andrews says, "No, Brit. Let her be."

Upstairs, I press my face hard against the bedroom window. No blue lights now, but the cruiser's still there. And the other car as well. Goo drips out of my nose and smears the glass. Drops run down my chin and fall to the floor.

The spasms fade and become hiccups. My heart still thumps, but my breathing slows. When the darkness passes, I wash my face and walk back downstairs to the kitchen.

The US marshal is still there. I look into eyes that proclaim the tender love of a father for his child. Almost, the man convinces me. Almost. But a chill shakes my body. None of this can be real. Why would Pasha do this?

I tap the guy's papers with a fingertip. "I'm that Anya. Guess you adopted me." My diaphragm contracts again—once, twice. I breath deep a few more times before continuing. "Except that Pasha and I switched places. So you got her instead of me. I went into foster care as Praskovya Kyrillovna Gilyova."

The man's face turns all sad, but determination still fires his eyes. "When I adopted you, you told me that your real name was Praskovya. I tried to find a birth certificate—any evidence at all that you were telling me the truth. There wasn't any. And your mother verified that you were her only child."

Mamochka what? No. She wouldn't. And—anyhow—I'm not the girl he's looking for. I reach across the table and pick up my sister's Ohio ID. "This says five foot one. Blue eyes." I set it down in front of the man. "Doesn't it bother you—just a little—that I'm five seven and have green eyes and red hair?"

He sighs and looks down at the table. Seconds pass before his eyes meet mine again. "A year ago, you looked like this. Exactly like this, Anya. It's your photo."

A casual shrug lifts my shoulders. "I saw Pasha yesterday. She still has blonde hair and blue eyes." She's still petite and feminine. Like I was. "A year ago, I was here. In foster care."

My bestie nods agreement. Her mother stands. "I'm sorry, Mr. Koshkin, but Anya's not your daughter. Brit and I have known her for about eighteen months."

Mr. Koshkin slides his chair back. Clouds pass across the man's face. "There's an exceedingly rare disorder that appears every few generations in my family. It's fatal if not treated early." The guy smiles, but his disappointment penetrates to my soul. "The initial symptoms are rapid growth and a change in eye color." He picks up his papers and tucks them back into his briefcase. "We adopted you from the only other family known to have the condition. Because you're at risk."

He drops a business card on the table. "Please come home, Anya. Don't be a fool." The man turns, walks down the hallway, and steps outside. I run up the stairway to watch his car leave. What's going on, Pasha? Should I have trusted him? Gone home with the man?

Familiar arms slide around my waist from behind and draw me tight. Brit leans close and whispers, "You'll be fine." My bestie—always the optimist.

The morning passes quickly. Though we make it to church on time, my brain refuses to think about anything but Mr. Koshkin returning with a warrant. For me. Even though I'm not his daughter. Then he takes me to doctors who know nothing about my intersex body, but who want to make me normal—whatever that means. Surgery. Hormones. I won't even have a say about which sex I'm to become.

After church, we drive back home and eat. I clean up the dishes and walk upstairs to the work room. To relax. Brit's in her bedroom, reading. Her mother's resting. I can paint in undisturbed silence. And dream of a future that will never exist.

Watercolors provide one of the few bright spots in an otherwise dismal life. With the sewing machine stowed, I use the flat top for my work surface. After a few minutes of deep breathing and relaxing my muscles, I begin touching up a portrait for Brit's birthday. Some-day soon I'll see my bestie smile.

Or not. The problem with watercolors is that you have to get the lines and shapes and colors right the first time. Unlike oil painting, it's almost impossible to make changes without ruining the entire thing. Which I just did. Again.

Okay, so I'm not the best painter. I get that. But I learn from my mistakes. And I keep trying. I drop my latest failure into the trash and clean up my mess. I stare out the window for a moment while the disappointment fades, then say goodbye to my bestie, walk down the stairs, and step outside again.

The Andrews home in New Brighton is about twenty minutes from Brush Creek Park by car. The Randall house in Beaver Falls is only about two miles away, though. So I walk home.

On the New Brighton side of the 7th Street bridge, the road splits into two one-way streets—3rd Avenue eastbound and 5th Avenue westbound. On the Beaver Falls side, the road is 7th Avenue. Beaver Falls and New Brighton both have a 7th Street, but neither one goes anywhere close to the 7th Street Bridge. Makes perfect sense to me.

I walk, though my body longs to run. Before the changes began, I wasn't into sports. Now I play soccer and basketball. So I can have peace from the constant desire for motion.

Most of the girls on my basketball team are taller than me. I'm stronger, faster, and more agile, though—at least in bursts. Playing soccer with the boys isn't about competition. It's about hiding just how much faster I am than any other girl—and most of the boys my age. I know what happens to intersex girls who are too good in sports. And—yeah—when I'm playing soccer, it's cool that people think I'm a boy.

Minutes later, I walk up the short driveway to the Randall home. Although I've spent eighteen months in the cedar and brick split-level, it's never felt like home. Yeah, the Randalls treat me like family. But we all know it's temporary.

I walk straight to my room, slide the storage box out from under my bed, and open it. A sigh works up out of my gut. My orien-tal landscape is safe. Not that it shouldn't be.

The fantasy watercolor is my best work, but I need to improve my technique before I dare to finish it. And that means adding gouache or acrylics over watercolor without making a mess of the underlying image. Some day I'll learn how. Some day.

The cherry trees have haunted me since they first appeared in my dreams. And the blonde-haired girl who wanders among them. A braid hangs down past her waist, white at the tip. She's alone, waiting for someone who never shows.

My foster mother taps on my door and walks into the room. I close the storage box, slide it back under the bed, and cross the room to greet her.

"I'm sorry," she says, pulling me into a tight embrace. "Lance Martin stopped by today. He says they're issuing a No Contact Order to Clara and Bridgitte Andrews. I'm not supposed to let you see them again."

I pull away from her and sit down hard on the edge of the bed. My life blood runs down my legs and forms a dark puddle on the floor. Nobody sees it. Nobody cares. But my life's over. 'Cause I won't survive without Brit.

"No more boys' soccer either," she says. "No more Anatoli. I'm sorry, Pasha, but no pretending to be someone else."

"My name's Anya." I bite down hard on my lip. A hundred times, I've tried to explain it all to her. The answer's always the same. As my foster mother, she has to do what the people who have legal custody want. And family services insists on going by the birth certificate they have for me—Praskovya Kyrillovna Gilyova. Pasha. My sister. Not me. Does it matter? My body's not Anya's anymore, either.

A soft rumbling outside reminds me of a promise I made. "All right," I say. Then I stand and kiss my foster mother on the cheek. "I promised Dylan I'd ride out to Brush Creek Park. That's probably him."

Mrs. Randall's eyes scan the ceiling. Like she's watching a video recording of Lance Martin's visit. Finally, she nods. "All right. You can go. Encourage him to call you Pasha, though."

Yeah. Like that'll happen. The boy loves Anatoli. Not some girl he doesn't know.

The doorbell rings, so I rush down the hallway and pull open the front door.

Chapter Three

Dylan gives me a quick hug before leading me to his motorcycle. It took me weeks—as Anatoli—to be comfortable around the boy. And even longer to risk being alone with him. He's never hurt me. But the old fear stirs anyhow. My heart thumps uncertainty. But I take the helmet he hands me, slip it on, and climb on the bike behind the boy.

I slide my arms around Dylan's waist and draw myself tight against his back. Like I've done on a dozen rides before. This time's more sensual somehow, as though we've crossed some imaginary line between friends and potential lovers.

The four-stroke engine purrs quietly beneath us as we pull out on the highway. A memory flashes by then—me and Papa riding Misty across the pasture and through a stand of ancient oak trees. On a day he wasn't drunk. When even my red corduroy overalls were okay with him. Till we jumped a hedge row. And I screamed. He reined Misty to a stop, his face gone dark with anger.

I close my eyes in a panic. Till my chest stops pounding. And the image fades. Shaking, I snuggle closer into Dylan's warmth and strength. My breasts press easy against his back. No binder now. No hat either. No hiding who I am.

The miles flash by, a blur of asphalt beneath—trees and blue sky above—till memories of Papa are lost in the distance. Till at last we slow down and turn into the park.

Dylan stops his motorcycle under the limbs of a giant maple beside the stream. I climb off the back, ease off my helmet, and shake my hair free. Dylan loves Anatoli. So why am I here? What's he want with Anya?

I sit on a boulder with my feet dangling over the creek and the sun warm against my back. Dylan perches beside me. After a moment, he slinks an arm around my shoulder and draws me close. Gay or not, he mimics perfectly the straight boy out with a new girl-friend.

I play along. Why not? Isn't this what everyone expects?

Dylan even does a timid first kiss. On the cheek. And slides a hand down to my waist.

I lean my head against his shoulder. Too bad he's so butch—at least physically. He's a good friend, but I'm not sure I'd want him as a lover.

Dylan's face turns serious. "Last month, my parents gave me an ultimatum—stop seeing you or move out of the house." He throws a pebble down into the water, then picks up another. "So, I took them to a Tigers game."

Yeah. My basketball team. How long has he known about that?

"Praskovya Gilyova," he says, "Pasha—a girl." His eyes wander out toward the stream again. "I had to explain why I never told Anatoli that I knew."

So I made the team because the captain had a crush on me. "Dylan, it's okay to love Anatoli." And not me.

"Not according to my father." He brushes a stray lock from my eyes. "And you deserve someone who will love you as you are—Anatoli or Pasha."

I kiss the boy's cheek. "It's complicated, but my real name's Anya. Pasha's my sister. We switched places."

The boy laughs. It echoes through the trees. "Another name. Why not?"

I lean my head against his shoulder and watch a family of chip-munks play on the far bank of the stream. For an hour—maybe two—Dylan seems content to just hold me. For an hour—maybe two—life isn't headed for disaster.

But clouds gather overhead. Wind rustles the treetops. A drop here. Another there. Soon the storm will break over us. Dylan hops up off the rock and helps me to my feet. "Let's grab something to eat. Okay?"

A raindrop splashes against my cheek and runs down my face. Soon enough, we'll be drenched if we don't move on. I take the hand he offers and rush back to his bike. "After we eat, can you take me someplace far away?"

"Why? What's wrong?" The boy's eyes overflow with tenderness. Yeah, Dylan loves Anatoli. Okay—maybe Anya too.

Hopelessness overwhelms me for a moment. "Family services says no more Anatoli or Anya. No Brit, either. I'm gonna die if I stay here."

Dylan's eyes turn dark. He shakes his head, and then pulls me into an overwhelming bear hug. No guy has ever done that to me before. After the boy releases me, he starts the motorcycle again. I slide on the seat behind him and pull myself close.

Hope he's not as crushed about this whole thing as I am. But it's not like I expected to suddenly be straight and have a normal body.

Half an hour's ride brings us to Melody's Diner—the place Anatoli and Dylan always stop for lunch and a long chat. I ease off the back of Dylan's bike and survey the clouds. Heavy rain's coming. Soon. Guess outing myself to a waitress at a country dive is better than getting caught in a thunderstorm. So I walk inside and hope Mrs. Andrews is still praying for me.

No customers in sight. The waitress looks up from wiping the counter. Melody greets me with something between a smile and a rude stare. I take a seat at the bar in front of her. "My real name's Anya. I'm intersex. And a girl."

Dylan kisses me on the cheek before taking the stool beside me. "She needs Grace's help," he says.

Melody disappears and returns a moment later with a coffee and a Coke—our usual—and a cup of hot water with a bag of tea. She eyes me for a moment—uncertain like—emotions flicking across her pretty face.

Then she turns to Dylan and waits till the boy sighs and nods his head. "I'm serious, Mel." He takes a sip of his coffee and smiles at me. "Melody here's got an aunt who helps place LGBT kids into accepting homes."

The girl nods, like that settles everything. Like it's that simple.

All I want is a family that loves me. Me—Anya. With whatever body and gender I've got. Like the Andrews do. Just a mom and a sister would be fine. Don't need a dad. But the system doesn't work that way. "If I run away, they'll just send me back here." And maybe lock me up.

"No, Anya. They'll transfer your case files and find you a real home." Melody takes a long sip from her tea, but her eyes never leave mine. "If you like, I'll call her. Once she knows your situation, I'm sure that she'll help."

"Now?"

"Yes. Now."

"Where is she?"

"Erie."

"I can't." Cold air flows down my spine. Muscles spasm. Terror drives me off the stool and across the room. Till I stare out the plate glass window at the rain and the wind and the angry clouds, expecting to see Papa's face.

Dylan eases close. "What's wrong?"

With me in the boy's arms, the darkness fades. Minutes pass while I hide from my own memories. "I was born there. When I was twelve, Mamochka—my mother—took me and fled south to get away from Papa's abuse."

I slide out of Dylan's embrace, grab a napkin, and blow my nose. "We were so happy back then. Till Papa found us." A flood of memories threatens to overwhelm me. So I stare at the driving rain again. And wait.

Melody walks around the end of the bar and stands beside me. Her reflection in the window displays a gentle smile. "The people my aunt works with are in New York State somewhere. When you're adopted, you can change your name. No one will ever find you."

He will. That fear will torment me for the rest of my days. If I let it. Terror still circling me, I nod at Melody. "Would you find out for sure that she'll help?"

The girl's hazel eyes study me for a moment before she walks back to the bar, digs a phone out of her purse, and calls her aunt. "Hey, Grace. Melody. Got a minute?" She turns toward me and smiles. "Yeah. I'll be brief. Got an intersex friend in foster care who needs your help. Can I bring her to you?"

The girl takes a sip of her tea—cold by now. "Great! I'll let her know. Thanks. Later." Melody walks back over to the counter. "She can see you Tuesday afternoon. I've been wanting to visit a friend in Erie, so I can give you a lift." The girl drops her phone back into her purse. Just like that.

"Day after tomorrow?"

"Yeah. At noon I'll be parked at the bank on Eighteenth Street."

"Wow. That's kinda fast." No chance to say goodbye to Brit.

"It's all right if you change your mind. I need to make a deposit anyway. It's fine if you don't show. No pressure." Yet her eyes insist I be there. Like it matters to her. A bunch. After a moment, her waitress smile returns. "So. The usual ?"

This place really does make the yummiest burgers. Dylan and I find our way to a lonely booth. Not our usual one, but back in the corner where we can talk in peace. The boy motions for me to sit, and then slides in beside me. Like a boyfriend might. Is he gonna insist on payin' for my meal?

Dylan intertwines his fingers in mine. "This is all pretty surreal for me," he says. "And way too fast."

Then slow down. I ain't the one pushin' this relationship. But I keep my mouth shut. Because—well—I'm not sure what I want from the guy at this point. Him caring about me feels good.

Melody interrupts the silence with our burgers and fries and fresh drinks. Her grin reminds me of Mrs. Andrews. Like a mother watching her daughter with a boyfriend. Sweet. I stare out the window again. The last few drops of rain draw expanding circles in the puddles. The sun peeks through the gray clouds overhead.

Anatoli and Dylan always talk about soccer. Now, neither of us know what to say. Dylan sets down his malt. He bites his lower lip while his eyes consider mine. "Come back from your adopted family long enough to go to the prom with me."

Wouldn't that be something? Seeing Ben react to an obviously female me. Yeah, kid, you got trounced at soccer by a girl. If Mamochka were alive, she'd love for me to go to a fancy party with Dylan.

The prom would be fun. A mischievous smile creeps across my lips. Brit's a Junior. Maybe I could dance with her too. At the least, she'd do my hair and makeup. Her mother would pray that everything goes well. Even the telling off Ben part. She'd laugh about that. She ain't perfect, you know. I inhale deep of the aroma of burgers and fries, then lean close and kiss Dylan on the cheek. "Let's do it."

Chapter Four

Monday morning dawns too early. Forgot to set my alarm. Have to rush outside without makeup or even my hair brushed. Whatever— it's raining anyhow.

Brakes squeal as the bus rolls to a stop in front of us. Lights flash red. The doors fold open. Water drips from the overhead frame. Heather closes her umbrella and steps into the bus. I follow. My foster sister glances back at me before sitting with her best friend. I find an empty seat two rows behind her.

Rain patters against the window beside me, washing away my dreams one drop at a time. At the next stop someone slides in beside me. I don't even look up to see who.

I'm not stupid. Okay? Not gonna run away to Erie. No matter what Melody says, nobody cares that much about an intersex girl. Nobody. Except Brit. And her mom. So I'm stuck here. Somehow, I gotta convince the court to let me see my bestie again. That ain't gonna happen, though.

A pained sigh lifts my shoulders. Somebody thinks seeing Brit is bad for me. Probably because she's gay. And out. And I'm not.

Okay, so we kissed. But it's not like we're a thing.

At school, I step off the bus into a cold puddle. A chill breeze pushes through the bulky sweater I borrowed from my mother. I rub at my itching bra and walk up the sidewalk into the building.

At my locker I grab my books and check for text messages before stowing my phone.

FosterOfTwo >> PKGilyova — Sorry. Forgot your appointment.
  Sophie out front at 8:50.

The air grows thick and warm. My lungs struggle to get enough oxygen. I lean against the wall for support. I'm doomed.

Through an open mouth I draw slow breaths. One. Two. Three. Till the darkness passes.

The psychologist was bad enough. My pediatric gynecologist is gonna know what's up. And too many of my online intersex peeps have been forced into treatment they didn't need. I just want to be left alone, okay? But the doctor probably won't do much today. Ask questions. Draw blood. Maybe prescribe some medication. I can still leave tomorrow if things go bad. Escape this worthless life. Find a forever family that will accept me as I am.

Geometry flashes by. I walk outside to see if Sophie's there. Yeah. Mrs. Zosia Wierzcholska—my Court-Appointed Special Advocate. The one person in the foster care system who listens to me.

But even she will betray me. Kids in juvenile court have no Constitutional rights. None. Not even attorney-client privilege. The judge decides based on what family services, my court-appointed attorney, and my CASA volunteer all think is best for me.

Her Kia's waiting. So I slide into the passenger seat.

The lady smiles back. "Hey, Anya. You okay?"

"I'd be better if I could stay with Brit's family."

"Yeah. I know. They think she's a bad influence."

"Because we're gay."

The woman glances at me and then nods. Guess I'm out now.

Seventh Avenue—Route 18—takes us across the Beaver River into New Brighton, and then south, across the Ohio River into Monaca.

As soon as the car stops, Sophie turns to me. "I can wait here. Or in Doctor Wilson's office."

Dr. Pamela Wilson. Pediatric gynecologist. If she does a pelvic, she'll know I'm intersex.

CASA volunteers have access to everything. Every last detail of my life. She's gonna read whatever Dr. Wilson puts into my medical record. "I want you in the room with me. The whole time."

The woman shakes her head. "They don't ordinarily allow unrelated people to be with a patient during an exam." Her eyes carry doubt, though. And a hint of rebellion.

"Sophie, my future depends on what you tell the court. You need to be there."

Her head dips in an uncertain nod. She gets it.

We sit in the waiting area for almost an hour before someone leads me down the hallway. They don't allow my CASA volunteer to follow. Oh well.

The doctor's assistant hands me a pink robe. "Open in front," she says. "Nothing underneath." After she leaves, I toss my things on the chair in the corner, put on the robe, and wait on the examining table.

I close my eyes and focus on Brit. For a moment, I see her through someone else's eyes. The girl's as unhappy about all of this as I am. Perhaps more so. If I'm ever gonna see my bestie again, I need to pretend I'm an adult. At least for the court.

An hour passes before someone knocks on the door. Dr. Wilson enters, along with a nurse. My CASA volunteer follows, a grin of triumph curling her lips. I smile at the woman and nod a thank you.

Dr. Wilson steps close to me. "I'm sorry, Pasha, but the court wants a complete physical."

I can be brave. For Brit. Yeah. For my bestie.

The doctor nods to Sophie. My CASA lady moves to the other side of me. Where she won't see my body parts, but can watch what's going on. And close enough to hold my hand. Yeah. Sweet.

Dr. Wilson looks into my eyes and ears. She uses a tongue depressor to check out my mouth. The woman presses the sides of my throat. She hits a couple of my joints with a small rubber hammer.

"You've lost some breast mass?" she asks. When I nod, she searches for lumps. There aren't any. She even presses her fingers up under my armpits. Nothing there either. After she listens to my heart and has me cough a couple of times, she sighs. "Everything appears to be normal thus far. Please lie down."

Sophie lets go of my hand and finds something interesting outside. As soon as I'm on my back, the doctor starts pressing various places around my abdomen and under the edge of my rib cage.

Several times, she slides a fingertip along the purple line that runs from my belly button down to my pubes. Then she shakes her head. "Did you have surgery when you were young?"

"Not that I know of. It's always been there."

She examines it one more time and nods. "All right. I don't think it's a concern." Then she sighs. "You should have more than Tanner 2 pubic hair development, though"

Yeah. The fine blonde down between my legs used to be thick and curly.

The woman nods toward the end of the table. "I need you to put your feet in the stirrups and slide this way. Yes. Like that."

When I'm in position, she covers my lower half with a sheet. "This shouldn't take much longer," she says. "Spread your knees for me."

My bravery crashes. The room turns freezing cold. I do as she asks, but my legs begin shaking. Gotta get out of here. Now. I raise my head and look at the door, then jump when someone puts a hand on my arm. Sophie. Yeah. Her. Gotta chill if I want to see Brit again. Chill. Seriously.

I flinch when the doctor spreads my labia. I am like way sensitive down there. Okay? My clitoris sticks out past my labia maybe half an inch. That's enough of a threat to the space-time continuum. I don't need it standing at attention with my doctor watching.

"You've never had vaginal intercourse?"

"No." Not even close.

"I'm going to use a speculum now. To take a look inside."

The muscles in my legs pull tight. My back arches up off the cushion. My elbows press hard against the table. All before she pokes the stupid thing inside me. Yeah. You girls remember that first time. I'm so tight that it's all about the pain.

Then Dr. Wilson slides it back out and wipes the gunk off my labia. "All right," she says. "I'm finished. When you're dressed again, open the door and someone will show you to my office."

A moment later I'm alone. I swing my legs off the side of the table, sit up, and pull the robe tight around me. Ten minutes pass, and my body's still shaking. I breathe through my mouth. Deep breaths. Slow breaths. Till my heart goes subsonic again.

Muscles twitch as I pull on my jeans and sweater. I brush out my hair, then take three more deep breaths before opening the door.

Eventually someone notices and leads me to a room with a desk, several chairs, and lots of books on shelves. Sophie and Dr.

Wilson sit across from each other. My CASA lady waves me toward the empty chair beside her.

The doctor nods at me. She runs a fingertip down the screen in front of her, then removes her glasses. "If you were eleven and had grown three inches, I wouldn't be overly concerned. At your age, however, six is rare. Exceedingly so."

She looks at Sophie like she might say something, then turns back to me. "When did you get your first period?"

Menstruation wasn't pleasant, but it meant I was a normal girl. "The summer between sixth and seventh grade. I was twelve."

"And your most recent one?"

Yeah. That question. I almost lie to the woman. Almost. But I'd be ashamed if I ever saw Mrs. Andrews again. And I don't want to fail her. Ever. So I tell the truth. "Six months ago."

One eyebrow rises up the woman's forehead, but she nods. Like she knows what it all means. "Are you on birth control?"

"No, ma'am."

"Are you taking hormones? Steroids perhaps?"

"No. Just my asthma meds."

Dr. Wilson puts on her glasses and types in something on her computer. "There's a doctor in Pittsburgh—an expert on intersex. I'm going to recommend that you see him. Corrective surgery is in order, but only after your diagnosis has been settled."

When I shake my head, she removes her glasses again and leans toward me. Determination lights the woman's eyes. She went to medical school. I'm only a kid. What do I know about my own body? Or my gender. Or whatever. So I keep my mouth shut. And breathe deep of the silence. Dr. Wilson's shoulders relax then. She nods. "Your foster parents thought you might have gender issues."

"Why? Because I played on a boys' team? The girls would freak out about how good I was."

She leans back in her chair. "Really? And to what do you attribute being so much better than they are?"

"I'm faster and stronger. Does it matter?"

"You might have high testosterone levels. We can test for that. But it sounds like your parents are more concerned than you are."

"Well, yeah."

The woman eyes me again, and then shrugs. "You do seem healthy enough. Let's run some blood tests to verify that. Okay?"

That's it, and I'm outta here? I nod.

Sophie and the doctor stay in the office while one of the staff leads me down the hallway to another room. There, a young man in scrubs asks me to sit in a chair. The one with a fold-down arm rest. For drawing blood. Yeah. That one.

The guy ties a rubber tube around my arm, cutting off the circulation. He tells me to clench my fist, though I'm not sure why. The dude sticks a needle into my arm. He's actually pretty good at his job. He finds the vein right away. Awesome. Then he pushes a collection tube into the syringe. The thing fills with blood. Except when he pulls it back out, the rubber stopper falls apart and the liquid spills all over my arm. Some of it drips to the floor.

The dude stands there, all wide-eyed, like something impossible just happened. Then the plastic part of the syringe crumbles. All that's left is the double-ended needle that's stuck in my vein. Tiny red droplets of blood drip on the arm rest. Some roll off and splash on the floor. Yeah, the guy's making a serious mess.

The man gently pulls the needle out of my arm and puts it into a medical waste container. He opens a little packet and uses an alcohol swab to clean the blood from my arm. But his eyes go wide and his body shakes. He removes his sterile gloves and shoves them into the medical waste. He eyes his fingers with a scowl. There's blood there too. He rushes to the sink, washes his hands, and puts on a new pair of gloves.

The dude stares at me while he has an asthma attack. Only his is way worse than mine are. The man starts gasping for breath and rushes out of the room.

Déjà vu hits me harder than it ever has before. A cute redhead says that our blood means death to humans. I yank the rubber thing off my arm, stand, and start pacing.

Ten minutes pass before another person in scrubs enters the room. She's pale. Like somebody just died. The woman motions me toward the door. "I'm sorry, but our phlebotomist has taken ill. You'll have to come back another day." Then she starts coughing.

I walk out to the waiting area. Sophie's talking with someone at the front desk, so I sit down and flip through a magazine till she's finished. On the way out to the car, my CASA lady says, "I'll let you see my report when I send it to the court. All right?"

"Yeah." When it's too late to change her mind. I slide into the passenger seat and buckle up.

As we cross the Ohio River bridge, the woman has a coughing fit. Then she glances at me. "Would you like to stop for lunch?"

And have to talk? "No. But thanks." Too many thoughts messing with my brain right now. Too many about ending it all. She's the last person that needs to know.

When Sophie turns the car into the driveway at my foster home, I almost change my mind. Almost. I sit there after the woman turns off the engine. Sit and wait for the courage to say something.

"We can go somewhere and talk," she says.

No. Here. Now. I take a couple of deep breaths. Slow my pounding heart. "You took away my best friend. My only friend, really. Now you want to mutilate my body. What makes you think I'll survive?"

Her eyes scan my face, trying to read my soul. But she's not Mamochka or Mrs. Andrews, is she? Can't see the mess inside. She reaches a hand across the seat and rests it on my arm. Like that's gonna help. "Whatever the judge thinks, you and Miss Andrews are good for each other. I objected to the No Contact Order and still do. But I think you need the surgery to have any hope of being adopted."

"Cutting off my clitoris isn't going to fix anything. Neither are drugs. No matter what they do to my body, I'll still be intersex."

The woman wheezes. Like the beginning of an asthma attack. She frowns and rubs at her chest. Then she stares at me for a moment before nodding. Her eyes bleed sympathy, but she doesn't think anyone else will listen. Yeah. I get that. So I nod goodbye and step out of the car, leaving behind my last hope.

After a late lunch, I walk down the stairs to my bedroom and spend the afternoon drawing a portrait of Brit. Or at least trying. The first three attempts end up in the trash. I set my pencil down before ruining the fourth and walk up the stairs to the kitchen to see if my foster mother needs help with supper.

"Thanks, Annushka," she says. "Everything's fine."

Not Pasha. Not even Anya. Annushka—the tender form of my name. A gentle goodbye, I guess. "I love you," I say and kiss her on the cheek. Then I walk back downstairs and finish my drawing.

Supper passes in silence. My foster-sister's eyes tell me she knows what I'm only guessing—I'm leaving for another placement soon. Within a couple of days. Better pack.

For a while, I let cleaning up after dinner numb my mind. But the sketch of my bestie waits for me, ready to be transformed into a watercolor. Or ruined by the painter. Yeah. That. But I want to make Brit smile, so I have to finish it and get it to her. Somehow.

I spend the evening on homework. I actually finish a paper for my History class. Catch up on my reading. Fold the laundry.

By nine, I'm out of excuses. So I return to the desk where I do my painting. I sit with my head in my hands, trying to decide what to do. Another pencil sketch? Watercolor the one with her smiling? I close my eyes and try to imagine how my bestie feels. Now.

Another hour passes. Brit's gone to bed. She's probably asleep. But when I look up, I see my bestie in her nightgown, sitting on the mattress with her head down. In her hands, she holds the heart Mamochka gave me. Yeah, I forgot to take that with me when I left. It's glowing again, a faint pastel blue.

Guess I'm the one who's sleeping. At my desk, dreaming of my bestie. Instead of painting. But the vision seems so real. I'm standing in the doorway to Brit's room. The house is quiet. I edge closer to the bed, careful not to disturb the moment.

My bestie's definitely not smiling. She hurts as much as I do. When I ease down onto the mattress, the bed squeaks. Brit turns toward me. Her eyes go wide. Her mouth opens, but only a little gasp comes out. She lunges toward me, but stops a breath away.

As in a dream, the girl returns my heart, clasping the fine silver chain around my neck. Then she starts crying. I pull her close and whisper my love in her ear. I hold my bestie while her shoulders convulse. Till her tears run dry, her body relaxes, and sleep takes her from me.

I beside the girl, my heart thumping. I've never had a dream this vivid before. Since I'm already wearing a long cotton nightgown, I lie down beside my bestie and follow her into the night.

Chapter Five

Tuesday morning creeps over the horizon as I sleep in my fantasy. My painting waits impatiently on the desk. For a few hours, life is perfect. The blonde-haired girl—the one from my dreams—makes sad eyes at me and shakes her head. She understands. Why can't people leave me alone? Let me be with my bestie. Yeah, I'm intersex. And she's gay. So what? We're sisters.

When I roll over, the bed squeaks a good morning. Like an old friend. Squeaks. Like Brit's bed. Yeah. Like that. I sit up, suddenly awake. Chill air and the early morning sun push through the open windows. The ones in Brit's room. Yeah. Those.

But Sophie dropped me off at my foster home. I sketched a portrait before supper. Ate. Helped mom with cleanup. Studied. Fell asleep while painting watercolors.

I wouldn't violate the No Contact Order. Get my bestie in trouble. I slide out of bed and walk to the doorway. My bare feet echo quietly through the empty house. Nobody's home—like in my brain. 'Cause I have no idea how I got here. One hand wanders up to my throat. Yeah. Brit returned the heart Mamochka gave me. Then cried herself to sleep. In my arms.

A glance at the clock tells me I'll be late for school if I don't leave soon. Brit and her mom are already gone. No time to figure out how I got here. So I find underwear in the dresser drawer. And my jeans. My embroidered peasant top hangs in the closet. Shoes? Yeah. Somewhere in the pile below, I find my sneakers.

I slip off the long cotton nightgown and put it away. I don't remember seeing it before, though it's a pretty vintage one.

As soon as I'm dressed, I head down the stairs. No time for breakfast, so I walk out the door and pull it closed. At the end of the driveway, I look back one last time. To be sure that I'm crazy. 'Cause things like this don't happen to normal people.

In the morning light, the water running beneath the 7th Street bridge beckons to me. As though I belong in its murky depths. I rush across and walk up 7th Avenue to my school. Then sit outside till the buses arrive.

I'm the first kid in the door, but find Dylan waiting at my locker. Dylan, who doesn't go to my school. "You okay?" he says.

I smile at the boy and shrug. "I need to see Brit again." Sorry, dude. Not you.

Tender concern flows from his eyes. "Maybe after you're adopted, you can come back and see her."

A hopeless sigh raises my shoulders. "I'm not going." I have to stay and face my issues. Somehow. "The judge in Erie would send me back. Or make me get surgery up there." Why would he care about some runaway? He's got hundreds of other cases.

I grab the books I need from my locker and start walking toward my first class. Dylan remains close beside me. "After what happened yesterday?"

"Dylan, I want to see Brit again. Okay? Even if I have to have surgery." 'Cause surrendering to medical treatment might convince them to let me be with her.

The boy pulls me to a stop. "They'll find you."

Kyrill? My abusive father? The one in prison? I stare at the boy like I'm an idiot. Which maybe I am. "Huh?" is all I manage to say. The bell rings, so I run down the hallway.

When Dylan catches up, he grabs my arm again. "Seventeen people died yesterday," he hisses. "And they're looking for someone with your face."

I step inside the room, late to Madame Foucault's class. Like I'll ever need French. But I sit through her lecture, trying to learn something. Anything to forget the morning's weirdness.

Geometry follows History. As I walk down the hallway to my Physical Education class, people stare at me and whisper to each other. They've watched me go from short blonde to tall redhead. Playing soccer with the boys doesn't make me transgender. Okay? Except it was fun being accepted as a normal boy instead of an abnormal girl.

Seventeen dead? The Zombie Apocalypse has taken Dylan. And Brit. My enemies too. They don't bully me any longer. Even my teachers avoid me.

My last class before lunch on Tuesday is Physical Education. I find an empty stall and change into my gym clothes. Even if I'm okay with having intersex junk between my legs, I don't really want the other kids freaking out. I've seen how people react to the possibility of a transgender student being in the locker room with the girls.

Ms. Farelli tells us to pick teams for softball. Nineteen girls in class today, so there's an extra player. But the coach waves me aside. Figures. She waits till the other girls leave before speaking. "I want you on the track team." I shake my head. Soccer and basketball are fine. I can hide my speed and agility in team sports. The focus isn't on me.

My teacher shakes her head. The woman's eyes insist that she cares. "Look, Pasha, I know you're fast. You should be proud of your capabilities."

I shake my head again. "When I win, they'll insist on medical tests. To make sure I'm female enough." And I'm not.

The coach's hands move to her hips. She was the one who pushed me into playing basketball. And, yeah, I love the game now. "Let me worry about that," she says. "Today, I want to see what kind of endurance you have."

Rather than argue, I shrug my shoulders. "Okay."

"How many lengths of the practice field can you run?"

"Wind sprints?"

"Basically. Distance is more important than speed, though."

Why not both? My muscles have been jittery all morning. I jog out past the middle school to the field, only to discover that the boys are using it for soccer. So I run beside the road. Back and forth. Again and again. At a slower pace than my body wants.

Cumulus clouds wander across the sky. My mind drifts to watercolors and oriental landscapes. If Melody's aunt found me an adoptive family, I could paint. Send Brit a present. Maybe even come back and see my bestie. Except that it's gotta be a scam.

Fifteen minutes later, I realize how many of the boys are staring. I force my body to slow down. Too late, though. Their coach waves at me. "You're Pasha Gilyova?"

"Yes, sir." I stop running and walk over to him.

A siren breaks the afternoon's peace. A large red truck turns off of Fifteenth Street, drives past us, and continues toward the high school. Beaver County Emergency Services. Special Services. Hazmat. The face of a pretty redhead flashes across my vision. They're here for me. Seventeen dead. I'm screwed.

After the vehicle passes, the coach turns back to me. "Ms. Farelli says you need to change clothes and report to the nurse's station." I look back toward the high school, to the field where the girls are playing softball. Coach Farelli stands near third base, but is looking in our direction. Yeah, I can see that far—one of the benefits of whatever is happening to my body. With a sigh, I start walking back toward the locker room.

"Never be ashamed of your body," the coach behind me says.

Two squad cars from the Beaver County Sheriff's Department arrive, blue lights flashing. One parks near the hazmat truck. The other closer to me.

In the distance, Ms. Farelli says something to the girls. They walk back toward the building. She remains near third base. "Run," she says—a whisper at this distance.

A couple of deputies get out of their cars and walk toward the school. The one closest to the doorway glances at me. "That's her!" he yells to his buddy, who's like twenty feet from me.

I run. Not fast enough, though. Something slams into my hip. Lightning flashes, and I'm on the ground and pulling at wires. The deputy lies on the ground, smoke rising from his body. Smoke! My brain makes no sense of it, but the other deputy draws a for-real gun and starts screaming for me to lie still and put my hands behind my back. Instead, I jump to my feet and run. Faster than anyone has a right.

I spend maybe ten seconds changing back into my jeans and top, then walk down the hallway and out the front door. No cops there yet. No cars at all. So I wander down the street to the crosswalk and find my way to the bank.

Chapter Six

Melody tells me to lie down in the back. Under a pile of blankets, in the warm darkness, I close my eyes and dream of an accepting family. Someone to fill the painful void left by the loss of Brit and her mother. I'll miss Dylan and Heather, too. Probably Ben as well. Eventually. Nah. Ain't gonna happen.

We drive for half an hour before Melody pulls to a stop. "You can move to the front seat now. And use the facilities if you need to."

Sunshine blinds me. I blink till my eyes adjust to the light. We're stopped at the Sunoco station on Portersville Road—the one out by the interstate. I stretch my arms and yawn, then fold the blankets and stack them in the back seat.

Soon enough, Melody and I are headed north on I-70. To Erie. And freedom. An hour—maybe two—and I'll be safe. Grace will find me a forever home.

We pass I-80—the snow line in winter—and Meadville. Melody turns off the radio as we approach Erie. "Grace works primarily with LGBT youth. That includes intersex, but I was wondering if you and Dylan were lovers. You don't have to tell me."

"No. That's okay. We're just friends."

"You're attracted to girls?"

"Yeah." I shrug and look away. "I've never actually had sex."

"Is it all right to tell Grace you're gay?"

"I guess so." Isn't intersex enough?

I-70 North becomes Bayfront Parkway in Erie. Sailboats, yachts, and the blue water—my eyes drink it all in. Not much has changed in the years I've been away, though only faded memories remain. On our left, an old smokestack rises—now only a skeleton of concrete and rust—all that remains of my childhood as well.

Melody turns into the library and parks. She digs through her purse for her cell and sends off a text message. "Grace is expecting us, so she shouldn't be long. Why not stretch your legs?"

Crisp air and blue sky greet me as I step out of the car. I breathe deep of the cold goodness and stretch my aching muscles.

Far up the hill and inland, an old church with golden domes watches over the city. Across Bayfront Parkway stands the hospital where Mamochka took me when Kyrill broke my arm. I stroll across the parking lot toward the library, enjoying the sunshine.

Loneliness gathers in dark clouds above my head though. If Grace finds me an accepting home, I'll still miss the Andrews family. Part of me wants to run back to Brit and her mother. But how long could I hide out with them? No. This is my best chance for a life. I wander back to the car.

A few minutes later, a dark-haired lady in a new Mazda parks beside us. Melody waves. "That's Grace. Wait here a minute." She gets out and walks over to her aunt. When she returns, she taps on the window and motions for me to follow.

Grace reminds me of the policewoman who took me into custody after Mamochka died—tall, thin, and muscular, determination in the set of her jaw. And a gentle smile. "I'm Grace Murrow," she says. "You're Anya Gilyova?"

"Yes, ma'am."

"Is that the name on your birth certificate?"

"It says Anna Kyrillovna Gilyova."

"You're female?"

"Yeah. Intersex."

"But your birth certificate says female?"

"Yes, ma'am."

"You're attracted to girls."

"Yes, ma'am." And at least one boy.

"All right. Let's find you a home."

Grace motions me toward her car, so I give Melody a quick hug, walk around to the passenger side, and climb in. Too easy. Way too easy. Life isn't this simple. Not for me, anyhow.

The woman pulls out of the lot, turns right on Bayfront and left on State, then drives up the hill past the hospital. At the next light she glances at me. "I need to stop by work for a few minutes. All right?"

"Sure." The sunshine and clean air are all I need.

She finds a space in a public parking garage on Ninth Street, and we walk into a white brick office building. The logo reads, "Erie County," but I miss the smaller print as we rush through the doorway.

The woman stops in at some secretary's office on the third floor. "Would you see if Stepan Davydov has an opening? My new client's a PREA risk."

The woman at the desk eyes me like I'm a juvenile delinquent or something. After a quiet phone conversation, she nods. "They're sending someone over."

As we ride the elevator back down, Grace leans against the wall and closes her eyes. "You know what a mandated reporter is?"

I'm screwed. "You're gonna turn me in."

That at least gets a chuckle out of her. "I'm required to follow certain procedures. I have to take you into custody. But we'll find you a good home. Isn't that what you want?"

"Yeah. It is. What's this PREA thing?"

"Prison Rape Elimination Act. A detention center's not the best place for an intersex girl."

An adult who talks to me like I'm a grownup. What a concept. But she's still gonna lock me up.

The door to the elevator slides open. I consider running, but only for an instant. Nowhere to go. So I follow the woman and hope for a future that probably won't happen.

In her office I crash in a chair in the corner. Instead of pacing. Instead of running. But my heart continues to pump adrenaline into my veins. Grace settles in at her desk and writes something on a notepad. Bits of quiet conversation drift through the doorway. Somewhere outside, a car honks.

Maybe twenty minutes later, a tall girl with curly black hair knocks on the open door.

"Jazmine! Come in." Grace walks around her desk to hug the girl. "This is Anya Gilyova, your new charge."

Dark eyes, lit with amusement, scan me. "Hey, Anya. I'm Jazmine Lamont."

"Hey." My escort can't be older than nineteen.

The girl drops into the chair next to me and begins rummaging through her bag. "Sorry, but we gotta wear a cuff while we're out. Policy."

Jazmine holds up a bangle bracelet, shows me an identical one around her ankle, and waits. After a deep breath, I hold out my foot.

It's not uncomfortable. Physically. But it means I'm a prisoner. I lean back and close my eyes. It's gonna be a long day.

The secretary from upstairs pokes her head into the office and hands Jazmine an envelope. "You're good to go."

Grace hugs me when I stand. "I'll be at your hearing."

"You'll place me with an accepting family. Right?" Me. Anya.

The woman nods. "Stepan Davydov will find you a loving home."

Jazmine snags my hand the way Brit always did. Like she owns me. The girl leads me down the elevator and into the parking deck to an old Chevy—one nobody would bother stealing.

We head east on Eighth Street, past State, where the road narrows. She drives a few blocks farther. Or maybe a couple of miles. I'm not paying attention to the scenery so much as studying the driver.

We park across from a place called Stepanova's, a two-story house that hasn't been painted in my lifetime. The first floor windows were long ago replaced by glass blocks. The painted image of a dark-haired woman holding a martini glass might once have added a bit of class to an otherwise seedy bar. The vintage clothes and hair style remind me of home. I turn my face away.

Jazmine takes my hand again and leads me up an iron stairway to the second floor entrance. "It's small, but..." She opens the door to a cozy but very nice apartment.

I follow her to a back room with an antique brass bed and a wooden chair but no other furnishings. "You'll stay in here," she says. "Stepan will bring you a dresser."

Stepanova—Stepan's daughter. He's her father? Tension bleeds out of my shoulders. At least I've got a decent place to crash.

The bathroom has a marble-tiled shower with glass walls, and a jetted tub big enough for two. Sweet. And a makeup table. A real one. I sit on the padded stool and roll close to the mirror. With the lights on high, I can see every last pore. Nice.

The kitchen is small. No. Make that efficient. It has all the modern appliances you'd ever want. Jazmine pulls open the fridge door. "Have you ever had a Frozen Russian?"

Alcohol? "I don't think so."

"They're lovely." Jazmine motions for me to sit at the kitchen table. The girl pulls vanilla ice cream out of the freezer—one of those small but expensive containers. Two large scoops go into the blender. From a cabinet, she gets three bottles. One's an Irish cream and another a chocolate liqueur. The largest bottle—a clear liquid— is unmarked. Vodka, maybe?

She pours the blended mix into two glasses. To one she adds several drops of fluid from a small bottle. "Most of Stepan's girls take theirs with a dash of vanilla. I like mine without." She places one drink in front of me and then sits down and sips at hers.

Stepan's girls. Too weird. Serving alcohol to an underage girl in a youth shelter. This whole thing has gotta be a prank. That would make Grace pretty cool, actually.

My drink tastes of vanilla, cream, and chocolate. And, yeah, alcohol. I savor every last drop as I study my roomie's face. Eyes, the loveliest dark blue. Clear skin a rich caramel. Curly black hair. A pretty flower graces her cheek—all soft pastel colors. I'm not a big tattoo fan, but this one suits her perfectly.

Concern hides in the tightness at the corners of Jazmine's lips. She's taking a risk on me. A runaway. Yet the determination in her jaw says it's her choice as well. I'm already family to her. But why, if they're gonna find me a home?

After we chat for maybe twenty minutes, Jazmine glances at her watch. "We need to talk about your work assignment, but why not refresh yourself first? There's a robe in the bathroom you can use." She rinses out both glasses and finds a home for them in the dishwasher. "Hand out your clothes, and I'll wash them."

Yes. Family. She tugs at my soul already. Like I've always had a crush on the girl. I walk to my bedroom and pull off my sneakers before heading to the bathroom. Blouse, jeans, bra, socks, and undies—I hand them all out to Jazmine in a bundle.

I lean back into the shower's hot embrace and let it massage away my tension. Shampoo suds circle the drain and carry my troubles with them. Things are gonna be fine.

A curious hunger grows. For Brit. Or Dylan. A desire for sex? Well, sorta. Maybe. Except that's insignificant compared to the need for someone to hold, and to share my dreams with.

A deep sense of peace washes over me. I pat myself dry and step out of the shower. For my hair, I find a blowdryer. Various cosmetics line the back of the makeup table. Foundation, rouge, eyeliner, lipstick—I run a fingertip across them all. How bad can this place be?

On shelves in one corner, with the spare towels, sit folded robes. Pink satin with ivory lace. Not as fancy as the vintage ones used to be, but still nice.

I find mousse in the cabinet and style my hair. 1950s. Audrey Hepburn. Then mess it up enough to make Jazmine wonder whether or not the effect is intentional. Yes. I can do sexy. I ease the door open and stroll out into the living room.

Jazmine's sitting in an overstuffed chair in the corner. A mischievous—almost wicked—grin creeps across her lips as she stands. The girl's wearing the same style robe as me. And it shows off her curves.

My eyes drift down to my own breasts and hips. Some part of my brain must be offline. 'Cause I don't know this Jazmine girl. I'm in some kind of detention center. Not on a hot date.

My new roomie approaches with confident grace. She tugs at my belt till it drops to the floor. "Let's see what we have here," she says. With tenderness, the girl spreads my robe. Not even Brit would dare such a move. But nothing in me resists. Nor even cares. I want to please her. But why?

"Nice." Gentle hands caress my hips, then slide upward till thumbs and fingertips measure my breasts. Her touch—more intense along my nerves than anything I've ever felt—slows time. This tsunami may never end.

Helpless, I yield to her. Was there any question that I would?

Jazmine's eyes seek out mine and hold me fast. One hand remains—as though it owns my body. The other moves lower. Wonder grows on her face. "You're intersex?"

I nod. Even if she were wrong, I'd agree just to please her. My need for human contact exceeds sexual desire, but both overload my synapses. Muscles tremble with frenetic—almost delirious—antici-pation. My breathing comes in shallow gasps.

I jump at a knock on the door. My chest pounds a crazy beat. The air around me crackles with tension.

The girl strokes my cheek, then kisses my lips. "It's all right, sweetie," she says. "That's Stepan and Dr. Campbell." Rather than answer the door, she leads me to her room and motions me toward the bed.

When I sit, she joins me, her hip tight against mine. That contact ripples through my soul. Fear joins the chorus, though. My body shakes. What am I doing here?

Jazmine pulls me close. "Don't be afraid. Dr. Campbell exam-ines all the girls Stepan acquires."

Acquires? Terror explodes, but only somewhere in the sparkling haze of distance. Too far away to affect my life. The two visitors pause at the bedroom door. Jazmine nods, then urges me to my feet. "This is Stepan."

The dark-haired man stands a head taller than either of us. His Russian eyes exude assurance and a tender concern. He throws a glance at Jazmine. "What do you think?"

She smiles at me and squeezes my hand. "Pretty, gynephilic, spirited, controllable. And intersex."

"Sounds like the supplier's description was accurate." He runs a hand over my hair, almost a caress. Even this stranger's touch brings pleasure. But my arms tremble. Supplier? What is happening?

Jazmine takes both of my hands in hers and leans close. "Relax. All right? The doctor's going to examine you."

I stare at the woman, mouth open. My arms cross over my breasts. I back up against the headboard. All but the most basic words fail me. "Anya," I say. Like she doesn't already know my name.

The doctor moves toward me. I slide away and take refuge behind Jazmine. The girl pulls me close long enough to whisper comfort in my ear, then helps me remove my robe and turn in a slow circle.

Stepan walks to a panel near the doorway. His finger hovers over a button. "Recording," he says, "She's all yours, Marie. I want options—the buyer will expect perfection."

As the doctor moves close, Jazmine steps behind me and slides her arms around my waist. Her chin presses against my shoulder. "I'm right here, girl. You'll be fine."

The woman checks my eyes, ears, and throat—the usual stuff doctors look at. My breasts and abdomen come next. With a scowl, she runs a fingertip down the purple line on my belly. "Yeah, that's always been there," I say, hoping that makes everyone happy.

Jazmine leans close again. "Now she needs to do a pelvic. All right, sweetie? You know the drill." The girl's voice comforts me beyond reason. With her hand guiding me, I lie on the bed and squirm my way toward the footboard. I raise my knees and spread my legs. My shadow flees from the woman's touch. My back arches in panic. Jazmine sits beside me again and runs a hand up and down my arm. "This won't take long."

Even with whatever happy juice the girl gave me, my muscles grow more and more tense.

The doctor pokes around my abdomen again. She pushes hard against each side of my groin. Examines my clitoris. "Intersex. You menstruate?"

"I used to."

"You went on birth control?"

"No. I just stopped. When my eyes and hair color changed." Our blood means death to humans. I bite my lip to keep from saying it.

Dr. Campbell examines my eyes more closely. "Russian ancestry?"

"Yeah. And Scottish."

"Your mother was Scottish? What was her maiden name?"

My eyes flick to Jazmine's face. She nods encouragement.

"Leannan Sìthiche," I say. Not sure why.

"No." The woman dismisses my answer with a wave of her hand. "That's not a name." She motions for Stepan to join her in the other room. A moment later, they both return.

The man sits on the bed next to me. He smiles like I'm his long-lost daughter. Tenderness flows from his eyes. "Are you sure your mother's name wasn't Koshkina?"

Ilya Koshkin—the US marshal—Pasha's adoptive father—I blurt it all out. Including what happened to the phlebotomist. Stepan just nods. Like I'm not insane. Like he already knows that my blood kills humans. Then he walks out of the room.

The doctor examines me again. Like she might have missed something. "You're the first one I've seen," she says as she writes something on her tablet.

Of a sudden, the spell dissipates. I pull on my robe, throw a wistful glance at Jazmine, and rush out of the doorway toward freedom. Straight into Stepan's open arms. He pulls my head against his shoulder. "It's all right, Annushka."

Even with Stepan holding me, I feel Jazmine's presence close by. "We're almost finished," she says. "Come back inside with me." A gentle touch from her peels me away from Stepan. She leads me like an obedient child back to her bed.

Stepan follows us into the room long enough to kiss first me and then Jazmine. "Don't push our little Annushka too hard."

"I'll be gentle."

The man's face turns serious. "No blood. Not a scratch. Nothing." After Jazmine nods, he walks out of the room.

The girl urges me onto the bed. We sit cross-legged, like we're at some pajama party. After a long silence, she takes my hands in hers. "The drugs I gave you heighten the sense of touch—the need for contact. They boost your sex drive, but only a little. And they render you more pliable."

My body trembles from the day's tension. Emotions run crazy. Jazmine's my only point of stability at the moment. My entire world.

She unties my robe again. Then hers. "Stepan wants to see how you perform with the dose I gave you. He needs to know how much you can handle." She nudges the robe down off my shoulders. "And what you like."

My body's ready to explode. I'll do anything she asks. Anything. If she'll just hold me. The light in the hallway goes dark. The outer door clicks shut. Desire surges.

Chapter Seven

Faded memories of a strange dream slip away as I wake. In the gray twilight of my room I stretch and moan. All I did was run away from home. Yet I feel like—like I had a for-serious workout. Or spent the night with Dylan. Yeah. That.

My leg cramps. The bed squeaks as I push myself upright. Jazmine gave me a ride to Stepanova's and showed me to this room in her upstairs apartment. Did I go right to sleep? Eat supper? Much as I struggle to remember, I dredge up nothing beyond an image of Jazmine's pretty smile.

The urge to pee drives me from the bed. I flip on a light and search the room. Nothing in the antique dresser. The closet is spot-less. And empty. My chest pounds syncopation. What did I do with my clothes?

A pink satin robe lies draped across the foot of the bed. A frag-mented image drifts across my vision—me showering and—I run fingers through my hair. Yeah. Mousse. But I'm out of time. I grab the robe and dash across the hallway to the bathroom.

After relieving myself, I turn the makeup lights on full bright and lean close to the mirror. No trace of makeup. Okay. Nausea whispers that—whatever happened—it's too late now. I should never have left my foster home. My heart thumps in my temples. What is wrong with me?

Jazmine's not in the kitchen or living room, so I tap on her door and ease it open. My throat tightens when I see her movie studio of a bedroom. Lights. Cameras. Microphones. Mirrors. A certainty not supported by memory strikes me—I've been here before. Naked. With her. Under the bright lights. Our bodies entwined.

Scenes from an old video flicker through my brain. The ache in my legs. The small bruises. Terror flows over me like the ocean breakers in a hurricane. I flee to the living room, but a dark-haired man with Russian eyes stands between me and freedom. Where did he come from? I gasp for air. My pulse races as I succumb to his overpowering grip. "Please don't hurt me!" I say. Almost a scream.

The man smiles reassurance. "Annushka. It's all right. You're safe here." He draws me close in a tender embrace and kisses my cheek. One rough hand lingers on my waist. His eyes insist that he'll protect me like his own daughter. Or some precious investment. A hazy memory fragment whispers his name—Stepan. Stepanova—Stepan's daughter.

I rest my forehead against his shoulder and give up any hope of escaping my insanity. But I long for some tangible sign of reality. "I can't find my clothes," I say.

"Jazmine will get you whatever you need." He kisses me on the cheek again and turns to go. In the doorway, he pauses and smiles before leaving. "You should rest."

An hour passes while I stare at the door and gather the fragments of my sanity. Jazmine brought me here. We were in her room together. Last night? The day before? How long have I been here? A tremor shakes my body—desire and loneliness. I have to get away.

When I touch the doorknob my foot screams in agony. I drop to the floor and grab at the cuff on my ankle, but my hands recoil from the pain. I roll on my side and draw my knees up against my chest. Seconds stretch to eternity before the pulses stop and the LED on my bangle bracelet turns green again.

Another hour passes—maybe two. I'm still staring at the door when Jazmine arrives. The girl's carrying a small cooler. When she notices me, her whole face warms. "Annushka! You're up. How are you feeling?"

I'm lying on the floor, you idiot. But my need for her surges beyond bearing. I push myself to my feet and struggle to remain upright. "I'm not sure," I say. I close my eyes against the desire to take her in my arms. "Like I was drunk but don't remember how much fun I had."

Jazmine sets the cooler on the kitchen counter before coming back to hug me. An electric thrill echoes through my nerve endings. I may not remember what we did, but my body bears the imprint of her touch, a mark more permanent than any tattoo. "Please hold me," I say.

"All right, Annushka. But you need to rest." She leads me back toward my bedroom.

Why am I doing this? I stop and pull away my trembling hand. "Where are my clothes?"

The girl slides gentle arms around my waist and draws me tight. "You don't need them."

There's no denying I belong to her now. My body, at least, knows the truth of that. The tremors stop. My breathing slows. "At least my necklace. Please? My mother gave me that."

She frowns disappointment at me. "I'll return your things once you've recovered. But you need to rest. Now."

Resistance fades. My body sways. "Okay, Jazmine. I surrender."

She leads me into my room and helps me into bed—like a mother with a small child. Before leaving, she drapes my robe over the footboard. "Stay put. I'll be right back."

I close my eyes, but sleep eludes me. Muscles draw tight. The bed squeaks every time I roll over. My heart pounds in my ears. Unable to think of anything but the girl, I push myself upright and sit on the edge of the mattress. Large drops of sweat run down my face and splash on the floor.

The door swings open—Jazmine in her robe. I lie down again, exhausted and breathing through my mouth. She slides beneath the covers and snuggles close. Her warmth stills the tremors. Eases the pain. My pulse slows. Sleep overwhelms me.

Chapter Eight

At least three days pass in the Stepanova place, and I still wake with the sheets damp from sweat. My body seems calm enough, though. I'm finally beyond the tremors and heart rumblings. My need for Jazmine's touch has made its own place of tranquility deep within my soul.

I roll out of bed and make my way to the bathroom. A hot shower eases the tension in my neck. As I'm drying myself, my roomie taps on the door and eases it open. "You have a court appearance this morning," she says. The girl approaches and slides warm fingertips down my arm. My heart beats faster—shouldn't it?—but the jagged edges of that first day have dissipated.

Jazmine nods satisfaction. "Blowdry your hair straight. No obvious makeup. The attorney wants complete innocence today."

"All right." But—hello—I still don't have any clothes. I grab my robe and walk back to my bedroom. In one drawer of the old oak dresser, I find my panties and bra. Having underwear feels oddly reassuring. Like I'm healthy again after a long illness.

I continue my search. A slip. Knee socks? Like I'd ever wear those. Three quick steps bring me to the closet. Inside, hangs a plaid skirt, a white blouse, and a forest green blazer. Miss Preppie? No way. I step out into the hallway—still naked—to find Jazmine.

"Can't I dress like a normal human?"

She smiles sympathy, but shakes her head. "The attorney wants to project classy and professional. No question of your innocence."

Running her fingertips down my cheek would decide the issue in her favor. We both know that, yet she treats me like an adult. So I give in. "All right. But I'll look like a twelve-year-old dweeb."

After I get dressed, I return to the bathroom to see about my makeup. Or lack thereof. A wicked grin spreads across my lips. Not dweeb. Cosplay. Well, she did say my makeup shouldn't be obvious. So I make my eyes larger and accent the little-girl cuteness of my mouth and chin. Then I use mousse to add a little spikiness to my straightened hair.

Before I go outside, Jazmine checks the GPS locator bracelet on my ankle. In case I jump out of the car and outrun both Stepan and his bodyguard. She offers me a warm smile. "Sorry, Annushka. Policy."

At least I get to go in a black limo. Like I'm some important criminal.

Eighth Street's one way to the east, so we drive into town on Seventh. The courthouse lies just off the square and looks kinda like the Parthenon. Stepan and his bodyguard escort me into the building. I sit in the deserted courtroom. The man takes a seat next to me, and his bodyguard sits closer to the door. His attorney arrives a few minutes later.

Then some young guy in a rumpled suit walks up to me and holds out his hand. "Miss Gilyova? I'm Robert Thornton, your guardian ad litem—your court-appointed attorney. Can we talk?"

Stepan nods when I glance at him, so I follow the guy to a private side room.

He pulls the door closed and motions for me to sit. "So you're a hermaphrodite?"

Why do I always get the losers? I stand and walk toward the doorway, but leaving's probably stupid. So I sit down again. "I've got XX chromosomes, a uterus, ovaries, and vagina. But because I also grew a large clitoris, I'm intersex."

"But you prefer to be a girl?"

You're missing a few cards from your deck, aren't you? "Something like that."

"How did you end up in foster care?"

"My dad got drunk, lost his temper, and killed my mother." The image of Mamochka's body lying in a pool of blood flashes across my vision. I've played through that scene so many times I know each frame by heart.

The lawyer guy gets up and paces. "So why did you run away?"

My blood means death to humans. Yeah. If they knew about that, the police would be here. So I talk about something more obvious. "Are you serious? Would you let somebody cut off body parts or give you hormones because they don't like you being intersex?"

The guy smiles like he understands. Or thinks I'm joking. "Yeah. I guess doctors don't always get it right."

"No kidding."

"And you want to remain with the Davydov family?"

"Do I have any other choices?"

He sits in the chair across from me and studies his hands. "You can go back home and see what the court decides. Not sure, but it sounds like you'd have to submit to your doctors."

"And have surgery."

"Perhaps. Or you can agree to whatever stipulations this judge has for giving the Davydov family custody and remain here with them until they find you a home."

His eyes scan me—once—twice. The guy knows something he's not saying. Something evil. Yeah. I get it. Seventeen dead. But the man just nods and walks me back to Stepan.

My new foster dad's chatting with Grace. She hugs me like I've always been her favorite intersex juvenile delinquent foster child. Then the woman slides an arm around my shoulder and takes me to another of the private rooms.

I slump into a chair and wait while Grace stares through the window into the courtroom. After a couple of minutes, the woman turns toward me. "Pasha, my department's not going to question your placement." She pauses for a deep sigh. "We will, however, encourage you to submit to medical treatment."

So she's read my case records. Or maybe Dr. Wilson's examination report. Or both.

No boys with breasts wanted. No girls with a too-large clitoris allowed. Somebody's gotta uphold the binary view of sex. Can't have hermaphrodites running around. So they erase us.

"Surgery," I say.

She nods, serious. "When you're ready." But her eyes say otherwise. Whatever happens next isn't my choice.

I follow her back to Stepan and try hard to act the proper young lady. Dark clouds gather around me, though. The need to be held surges, threatening to undo me. A tremor shakes my arm. Without even a glance in my direction, Stepan wraps his fingers around mine.

How many others have been here before me? How many have they screwed with their drugs? And then sold?

"Annushka." His voice—though a whisper—comforts me. "I will never let the doctors take away that which makes my daughter unique. I won't let them study you or put you in a cage. Whatever I promise the court, remember that. Will you trust me?"

"Yes, Papa." A cage. To keep my blood from killing anyone else. A tear breaks loose, runs down my cheek, and plops on my skirt. Part of me freaks at my insanity. This man will sell my body—I'm sure of it—yet he promises to protect me. And I believe him.

A door opens. "All rise!" The cop in front scowls at the small crowd till everyone is standing. "The Court of Common Pleas of Erie County is now in session, the Honorable Judge Rudolph Theissen presiding."

An older man in a black robe walks in, sits down, and nods at us. "Please be seated." He reads something on his computer screen, and then says, "Gilyova. Disposition."

With a feather-light touch against my back, Stepan urges me forward, to stand near one end of a long table facing the judge. My guardian ad litem and Stepan's attorney stand on either side of us. Grace approaches the bench and, after a few quiet words, walks back to a podium near us. There, she opens a fat notebook. "Your Honor, all parties are in agreement regarding custody."

The judge types something on his keyboard and looks up. "Why not send her back? We have enough cases without taking on one more."

"The child fled imminent physical and emotional harm."

One eyebrow creeps up the judge's forehead. "Medical treatment for intersex?"

"Your Honor, the girl has partially fused labia and a large clitoris, but is otherwise female." Grace walks up to the bench and hands the judge several papers. "Reports from Dr. Wilson and an intersex legal group. Decisions regarding surgery should be made by the patient and her doctors. Not family services or the court system."

He scans the papers and sets them aside. After typing something on his computer, he takes off his reading glasses and frowns at me. "You're a girl?"

"Yes, Sir." I show him my best smile and nod—pure cuteness. If the man sends me back, I'll end up in some kind of quarantine. Permanently. My hands shake so much that I hide them behind me.

The judge turns his attention to Stepan. "You're equipped to care for an intersex child?"

"Yes, Your Honor."

"Including all appropriate medical treatment?"

"Yes, Your Honor."

The judge's attention returns to Grace. "Petition granted. Interim custody to Stepan Davydov."

"Thank you, Your Honor."

Stepan winks at me, takes my hand, and leads me outside.

Chapter Nine

On the steps in front of the courthouse I lean against a fluted column and cherish the sun's warmth on my face. Stepan's not in any hurry. Neither am I.

Men in expensive suits greet him with respect, like he's somebody über important. A few speak Russian with the guy. And one—an older dude with a fancy cane—threatens him.

His bodyguard—closer to Stepan now than his shadow—seems overlooked by the crowd. I wink at him when he glances my way, but his scowl doesn't change.

When the limo arrives, Stepan motions me toward our ride. I skip down the steps like I really am a twelve-year-old dweeb. Our driver opens the passenger door, so I scoot across the back seat to the middle. After the car's moving, Stepan squeezes my hand. "I am proud to have you as a daughter, Annushka."

No man's ever said anything like that to me. Ever. "Thank you, Papa." Drops gather in my eyes. Whatever stupid drugs they gave me have totally wrecked my emotions. I turn my head toward the window and try to blink away the tears. Before my cheeks are dry, we're on the interstate heading east.

The people my aunt works with are in New York State somewhere. Just like that we leave Erie behind. One hand drifts up to where Mamochka's heart should be. Pressure builds in my chest. Breathing becomes a struggle. My pulse beats like a racehorse gone wild. Tremors shake my leg. A great drop of sweat runs down my nose and plops on my lap.

Stepan slides an arm around my shoulder. I press my face against his chest and grab handfuls of his suit coat. Muscles seize. My back arches against the pain. I gasp for air.

Strong arms draw me tight. "I'm sorry, Annushka. We'll be home soon."

After an eternity, the tension begins to fade, and my muscles relax. I lie exhausted in Stepan's warm embrace. When we finally stop, he carries me inside and lays me on a bed—a full-sized brass frame with a comfy mattress.

A younger woman in blue scrubs rushes in. She takes my pressure and temperature and blood oxygen level and all that. Then she pulls off my shoes and undoes the top two buttons of my blouse. Without a word, she leaves the room.

A storm gathers somewhere nearby. The pressure builds again. A muscle twitches. Tendrils of pain crawl across my scalp. I lie on my side and curl up tight.

Jazmine walks into the room and kneels beside the bed. "How are you feeling?"

I try to sit up, but the world spins me back down again. "Like I fell over a cliff, hit the bottom, and am still bouncing."

Jazmine gathers pillows from the chairs in the room and stuffs them behind my back. Till I'm sitting upright. Then she leaves. I brush a hand across my forehead to wipe away the moisture. A drop that I miss burns my eye.

Jazmine returns with a frosted glass. No. I want my emotions back. And my body. A single shake of my head is all I can manage against the need for her touch. Better the pain than slavery.

She perches on the bed next to me. "You can't quit cold turkey," she says. The girl's eyes insist that I can't quit at all. Ever. It's already too late. So close—her touch would bring relief. My muscles tighten. No. No more drugs.

Jazmine sets the glass on the nightstand. "One more dose after this. Then we switch to something milder." She reaches toward me. To run the back of a fingertip down my cheek. Like she has so often. Only this time, she doesn't touch me. "Please take it, Annushka."

And what if I do escape? Where will I go? I reach a shaking hand toward the glass and nod my acceptance. The girl holds the drink against my trembling lips. She slides close, till her hip presses against my leg, and my pain begins to ease.

When I can stand, Jazmine helps me undress. "Rest," she says. "I'll be back in about ten minutes. Stepan has a gift for you." She leaves me with a tender touch and a kiss on my cheek. Almost normal again, I pull back the covers and crawl into bed.

When Jazmine returns, she strips and drapes her clothes over the high-back chair in the corner. Once in bed, she snuggles up behind me. With a fingertip, she draws a line high across my cheek-bone. "You're one of us now," she says. "A Stepanova. Today you get your orchid."

Seconds pass before my brain gets what she said. "A tattoo?"

"Yes. From Stepan and Zinaida, a promise of their protection."

A tattoo was never on my bucket list. Especially one on my face. And I don't like needles. Really. I sit up and shake my head at her. "No, Jazmine. Just no."

Anger blazes in the girl's eyes, but she only sighs and moves closer. "All of the girls get them, Annushka." A hand on my arm, she brushes her lips against mine. "And I promise it won't hurt for long."

Twenty minutes later, the lights flicker on. The woman in blue scrubs stands behind a cart full of disposable medical stuff, bottles of ink, and one of those electric needle things.

My shadow leaps up off the bed and runs down the hallway, seeking escape. Yet I remain here, unable to overcome my desire to please Jazmine. My own fault for taking her stupid drugs. What would Brit's mother think of me now?

The sting of the needle isn't much, but the endless vibration of pain wears me out. Till a slow drop runs down my nose and splashes against the pillow. But I'm a Stepanova now. I belong to someone.

After the tattoo's finished, the artist covers her work with a layer of clear plastic. She applies a base coat of something like foundation, and then paints brighter pastels on top of that. Finally, she sprays a bit of some clear sealer over it all.

The woman leaves Jazmine and me in darkness. Alone. Though my desire burns deep, I lie still. Contact with the girl is enough to still the worst of my longing. And give my body peace.

Hours pass. My stomach rumbles. Beyond the windows, the sun rests in the distant treetops. Behind me, Jazmine stretches. "We should get ready for the party."

"With my face all swollen? You can't be serious."

"Oh, but I am." The girl slides a hand down my side to my waist. The other finds my one ticklish spot and drives me from the bed.

"Zinaida bought you a dress." Jazmine grabs my hand and leads me into the closet to one of the gowns—all pink and lilac and cream. Time slows to a halt. In a faded dream, Dylan and I dance in the school gymnasium. Has it only been a few weeks since the boy asked me to the prom?

Jazmine pulls the dress off the hanger and holds it up. Yeah. Tulle and satin and velvet—the dress Brit and her mom gave me. I check the bodice seams and underarms for the repairs I made, but find none. Not the same dress. I slide the gown over my head, wiggle it down, and zip up the side. Lovely fit.

Mrs. Andrews must still be praying for me. 'Cause there ain't no way this kind of thing happens at random. Not to me, anyhow. I spin around to see how the skirt flies. Perfect.

In the bathroom, I find makeup and mousse. My cheek is swollen and a bit red—not much I can do about that. But I add some rouge so the other side is pink as well. With my hair, I do a sort of redhead Marilyn Monroe thing—all smooth waves.

Jazmine walks into the bathroom wearing a slinky black dress. Like I need that distraction on top of the drug-induced craving for her. The girl smiles like a shark and presses her body against mine long enough to kiss my cheek.

"Come on, Stepanova. Let's show them what you've got."

With a hand on my waist, the girl urges me down the hallway and across the great room. Candles flicker in the subdued light. Flowers on the tables release their sweet perfume. A few guests look up from their quiet conversations as we pass.

Jazmine stops near a table where Stepan and two women are talking. The girl pulls me close and nuzzles against my ear. "Be sweet to both of these women. Zinaida's your protector. The other's a good friend of hers."

Stepan rises from his chair—as graceful as I've ever seen in a straight guy—and kisses me on the cheek. "Annushka, you look marvelous." Then he turns and greets Jazmine.

On the table between the two women lie photos. Of naked girls. I close my eyes and turn away. Who else looks like that between the legs? Shame floods me, though I remember nothing of what I did.

Jazmine slides her arms around my waist and draws me close. "It's all part of life's game, Annushka. A small price to pay for being a Stepanova."

But what's the point if living destroys my soul? I back away from Jazmine. Into Stepan. The man snaps his fingers at someone across the room. One hand envelops mine. The other perches on my waist. Slow dance music starts, and we drift out to the open floor.

I don't dance, okay? But he sure knows how to lead. So I rest my head on his shoulder and let the time pass. After a half dozen tunes, he leads me back to his table, pulls out the chair next to his, and motions for me to sit. "You're family now, Annushka."

So I pretend I'm a gorgeous redhead at a swank party instead of —instead of whatever you call my reality. One of the staff brings food. Fancy stuff I've never seen before. Probably tastes good. But I can't eat.

I look up to find the woman next to Zinaida fondling me with her eyes. Well that's what it seems like. When I return her stare, her smile only deepens.

For someone older than my grandmother, the woman's in remarkably good condition. She's tall and thin, but shapely. Her silver hair's cut in a rather boyish—but definitely cute—style. Still— too creepy.

After the main course, I excuse myself and walk back toward the bedroom. A little girl—who's maybe eight or nine years old— pops up out of her seat and runs to me. "Annushka!"

Her tattooed face echoes in a forgotten dream. My ears, at least, know her voice. Pretending I'm not insane, I pick her up. "Hey, sweetie! How have you been?"

A woman from her table approaches, so I put the girl down again. She runs to the lady and tugs at the hem of her dress. "That's Annushka. She taught me the new game."

The woman smiles at me. "Thank you for grooming her," she says. Then she picks up the girl and walks away.

I don't remember the kid. Or her game. But I no longer doubt what I'm capable of. Not with Jazmine's persuasion coursing through my veins. As my anger grows, a tear breaks free and runs down my cheek. I might deserve this. But not that little kid. I struggle to even imagine harming Jazmine, but my fists ball up anyhow. Spitting in her face might well cost me my life. But I don't care to live with myself any longer.

All I manage is a scowl and an icy stare. My body refuses to do anything more. So much for my bravery. I step outside into the damp air—away from everyone else. A pale moon sleeps with the diamond dust scattered across a silent black sky.

I untie the belt from my dress and slip it off. It should be strong enough. Closer to the pool, a pewter urn with two handles sits at the edge of the pathway. The thing's too heavy for me to carry, but I can tie my belt to it and roll it off the edge at the deep end of the pool. The weight should be enough to hold me under the water.

Three steps—that's as far as I get before pain lashes my ankle. Two more steps, and fire crawls up my leg. In a panic, I hop back toward the house, stumble, and fall. I can't do it. The pool's too far, the pain too great. How do I find Mrs. Andrews' God? To take me home. To Heaven with Mamochka.

I'm still lying on the paving stones when Jazmine comes for me. She says not a word, but takes my hand, helps me to my feet, and guides me back to our table. Zinaida frowns as Jazmine wipes the mud from my elbow. Her friend eyes me with curious sympathy. Stepan sets a glass of water and a couple of oval blue tablets in front of me. "This will help you sleep." he says.

Can I have a whole bottle of them? But I swallow his pills without complaint and let Jazmine lead me back to our room. The girl helps me out of my dress and into bed. She doesn't say anything at all, but holds me while I fade into unconsciousness.

Chapter Ten

The night brings chills and tremors, though I lie secure in Jazmine's healing embrace. Morning creeps into early afternoon before the girl slides away.

She returns with coffee and hot rolls. Cinnamon, brown sugar, and butter—the aromas drag me to a sitting position. I yawn and stretch before scarfing my breakfast. Funny how much caffeine and sugar can improve your mood. But, actually, I feel well rested.

My arm aches, though. I seem to have bruised my elbow pretty good. My hand wanders up to my cheek. I got my tattoo yesterday. We had a party. I push myself out of bed and rush to the closet. The nice vintage dress has small rips in the crinoline. And what appear to be mud stains. I turn around and search Jazmine's eyes for a clue. "What happened?"

Sadness flickers across her face, but she shakes her head. "Nothing to worry your pretty little head about." She kisses me till the tension drains out of my body. Then she grabs my hand and tugs me toward the door. "Let's go swimming."

No robe. No swimsuit. Not a string bikini. Just two naked girls walking past the staff and the guests and out the back doors into the afternoon sunshine.

A silver-haired lady sits in one of the cedar lawn chairs, sipping her tea. The woman's black bikini reveals a nice figure. Her body's too young for her to have gray hair.

Jazmine pauses in front of the woman. "Bonjour, Madame."

"Bonjour, jeunes filles." She lifts her sunglasses and winks.

Jazmine slides a hand across my back and down to my rear. See my pretty hermaphrodite. See her get aroused when I run my fingers up her hip.

I throw a pleading glance at Jazmine, but she grins and kisses my cheek. She nods at the silver-haired woman and leads me to the pool. Jazmine and I walk the shallow end, hand in hand. Though the cold water leaves goosebumps, the sun warms my back.

The French-speaking woman saunters toward us and perches on the edge of the pool. With her feet dangling in the water, she waves. "La fille intersexe—est-elle prise?"

Jazmine slides an arm around my waist and pulls my body tight against hers before answering the lady. "Pas encore, madame. Est-ce qu'elle vous plait?"

Okay, so now I'm wishing I'd paid more attention in my French classes.

The older woman nods. "Peut-être. Puis-je?"

"Bien sûr, madame." A beaming Jazmine tugs on my arm. "Come on. She wants to meet you."

Again? But I follow the girl to a ladder, climb out of the pool, and stand dripping on the tiles. The woman strolls toward us with the grace of a dancer. She must be close to six feet tall. Not masculine, though. Not with that body and those moves.

Jazmine squeezes my hand and grins at me. "Annushka, this is fantastic. Dixie is one of Zinaida's closest friends." The girl slides a hand behind my back and urges me forward.

The older woman's attention flicks down to my breasts—and further south—before resting on my face. One hand makes a home on my hip while the other explores. Like I need to be checked out by somebody's grandmother. Though my anger flares, not a muscle twitches.

The woman smiles like she already owns me, and brushes her lips against mine. Just like that. Blue eyes all but make love to me.

With a hand between my legs, she pauses and looks at Jazmine. "Est-elle fertile? Nous voudrions la féconder."

"Oui, certainement."

My body responds to the woman's touch. The drugs haven't left me any control, but I still blush. Okay, so I might one day consider myself a lesbian. Maybe. But that doesn't mean I'd sleep with some-body's grandmother—however pretty the woman is.

Dixie runs her fingertips over every last part of my body. Exam-ines my teeth even. And pokes at some very private places. I smile like a rabid dog, but don't quite snarl. Enough with the fondling already.

Amusement lights the woman's face. She kisses me again and turns to Jazmine. "Bien, combien coûte-t-elle?"

"Oh, elle est très chère, madame. Mais cela vaut vraiment le coup."

"J'espère. Nous verrons." After one last touch, she turns and walks back toward the mansion.

Jazmine leans close. Her smile dares me to object to what just happened—or anything else in my Stepanova life. The girl's proxim-ity sets off a wave of desire. Her face softens a bit then, and she runs a hand down the side of my waist. "I need to see Zinaida about this. Why don't you wait for me here? You could use a little sun."

The girl doesn't need to remind me that my life's been recorded —all of the things I've done in the past few weeks, but don't remem-ber. Would I hate myself more if I watched? I could blame the drugs, but what have I done to resist?

The sunshine warms my face, though the breeze chills. I settle into a chair, close my eyes, and pretend I'm somebody else—Miss Anna Andrews—on vacation with my mother and sister. With the drugs, I'm not sure whether or not I miss them. Not with every fiber of concern reserved for Jazmine.

An hour or two later, someone runs fingers through my hair. Jazmine sits on the grass beside me. Fully clothed. "Wonderful news!" she says. "Dame Mireille Dubois has agreed to adopt you." She helps me stand.

"Her?" No.

"Yes. Dixie's credentials are impeccable." Her hand clasped firmly about mine, the girl leads me back inside.

Compared to what? A mass murderer? I'd rather make porn. "No, Jazmine. Please?" I rush to keep up with her pace.

She stops inside the doorway and crosses her arms. "The contract requires that she treat you like her own child."

She probably molests them as well. I shake my head again in a panic. A sudden need for touch overwhelms rational thought. I reach a hand toward Jazmine, but for the first time, she backs away. "You ever had a man hit you for no reason?"

The voices whisper terror in my ears, but I take several deep breaths to calm my heart before answering. "Yeah. A number of times. Why?"

"Zinaida won't allow that to happen to any of her girls. For the first year, Madame Dubois has to bring you back here every three months for followup—to verify that she's treating you well."

A tremor shakes my body. Tiny flashes of lightning run across the edges of my vision. The storm begins. "No."

Jazmine squeezes my arm—to keep me from falling, but it lacks warmth. After a moment, she leans close. "That gentleman in the blue tuxedo—at the party—was Randy. Last month, he bought a thirteen-year-old girl. His daughter needed a heart transplant."

I don't remember the dude. Really. Nor even the party. Acid bubbles up out of my stomach.

"Another of the guests—I won't tell you which one—made a snuff video with the kid just before the doctors sliced her open." Jazmine's face softens. "Look, Annushka. I don't want you to spend the rest of a very short life in pain. Or at best, working the streets. All right?"

Last month, flipping them all my middle finger would have come easy. Now I struggle to gather enough strength to survive. My gaze wanders back to Dixie. "When?"

"You and I spend the night together—our farewell." She brushes a tender hand down my cheek. "Tomorrow morning, you're getting an implant—a milder form of the drug you've been taking. Then you'll accompany Dixie home." Jazmine leads me across the room to Zinaida. And my doom.

At a break in their conversation, Zinaida nods at Jazmine. "She's ready?"

"Yes. I think so."

Stepan gives us both an encouraging smile. "You do this willingly, my daughter?" he says.

I'm standing here naked. Jazmine just threatened my life. I've been drugged and seduced multiple times. Today, an old woman groped me. And you want to know if I consent to being molested by her? Insane laughter probably isn't the best idea. Neither is showing him a closeup of my middle finger.

So I nod instead. Fool that I am.

Is there any other choice? Rape. Torture. Death.

I think about prayer. Finally. But why should Mrs. Andrews' God help me? What have I done to resist? Nothing. And I got myself into this.

"Come on." Jazmine slides an arm around my waist and leads me back to our bedroom. She goes to the closet and picks out a dress. Something you'd wear going out with friends. Nice, but not formal. She kisses me—a quick peck on the cheek. "I took the liberty of ordering dinner for us."

Like I'm hungry. At all.

As soon as I've got clothes on again, Jazmine leads me back out into the great room, to a table in the corner. Away from where Stepan and Zinaida usually sit. Someone dims the overhead lights, and one of the ladies, in her kitchen uniform, brings candles.

And then drinks. *Have you ever had a Frozen Russian?*

Why not? I pick up the glass. No hint of vanilla. Not that it matters. I take a sip. Okay, more like a gulp. Jazmine grins and shakes her head. "Nothing more than alcohol tonight."

Has the girl ever lied to me? A sigh lifts my shoulders. She doesn't need to. Stepanova may own me, but Jazmine holds the keys.

After we eat hors d'oeuvres, someone from the kitchen brings a hot pastry roll. The woman cuts it open to expose mushrooms and meat—probably beef—with a dark gravy.

Jazmine grins at me again. "Beef Wellington," she says. "A treat." After the kitchen staff brings mashed potatoes and roasted Brussels sprouts, the girl moves from the other side of the table to the chair beside me. She eyes me with tenderness. Like we're lovers on a date. Instead of whatever you call modern-day slavery.

The food's yummy. I get that. And twenty minutes after finishing my first Frozen Russian—yeah I'm on my third now—I gotta admit that they're not spiked with anything more than alcohol.

After I finish off a piece of cheesecake, I lean against Jazmine and rest my head on her shoulder. She helps me to my feet, and I wobble back to our bedroom in her arms.

While I sit on the edge of the mattress, the girl searches through a drawer for something. After a moment, she returns with a small jewelry box, which she hands to me.

I look up into the girl's face. She's a bit unstable on her feet now. Guess she's not immune to the alcohol. I like her. Really. Too bad our relationship isn't my choice. Okay, so it's probably not hers either. Just doing the best with the hand she was dealt. Thanks, but I'd like to sit out the next round. Or two. I miss my bestie.

The girl sighs and reaches down to take the box from me. She snaps it open, shows me the silver chain and heart pendant. Yeah. Mine. The one Mamochka gave me. Looks like they polished it or something.

Without a word, Jazmine clasps the chain around my neck, then kisses my forehead and walks back to her dresser to get a night-gown. Warmth flows into me from the metal. For a moment, I'm with Brit again, comforting her. I cover the heart with one hand to hide its faint glow. A smile creeps across my lips.

A few minutes later, Jazmine and I are in bed, snuggled close, but drifting off to sleep. My hand still guards the heart at my throat.

Chapter Eleven

I wake to the aroma of bacon, eggs, and coffee—my favorite break-fast. Jazmine's already dressed and standing beside the bed. The girl hands me a platter. Yeah. Great. My last meal.

I spent the night—in my dreams—searching for a way out. To home or heaven. I pleaded with Mrs. Andrews' God. But I'm still here. The cavalry ain't coming. So I spend the rest of my life—however short—with an old woman as her sex toy.

All I wanted was a loving home. One that didn't care about me being intersex. Too late now, I guess. I roll out of bed and stand there naked. I know better than to ask for clothes. Jazmine kisses me one more time before we leave.

Dixie greets Jazmine and joins us as we walk down the hallway toward the clinic. Dr. Campbell is waiting there. She motions me toward an examination table. Dixie smiles and urges me forward. "Tu connais la musique, ma chérie."

Yeah. This tune I know. Slave or free, a pelvic's the same. Well, a little privacy would be nice. Dr. Campbell smiles at me and covers most of my lower half with a sheet.

My eyes go wide when she holds up a syringe. The woman sticks me in several places around my belly button. After she cuts a small incision, she picks up a blunt needle as big around as my little finger. My heart stops. Every muscle in my body tenses. I forget to breathe. The doctor inserts something into my lower abdomen and tapes the wound closed. Just like that.

Dixie squeezes my hand again and leans close to Jazmine. In a hushed voice she says, "Combien de temps avant que..."

Jazmine glances at the doctor. "Three months?" The doctor nods. She turns back to Dixie. "L'implant va durer trois mois."

Dixie shakes her head. "Ce n'est pas ce que je voulais dire. Le médicament est toxique, n'est-ce pas?"

Jazmine faces the doctor again. "She wants to know how long someone can tolerate the drug."

Dr. Campbell gives Dixie one of those classic impatient doctor sighs. "The medication eventually burns out parts of the central nervous system. Most girls last between five and seven years before we have to put them down."

Jazmine glances at me. "Entre cinq et sept ans."

The doctor's so nonchalant about my death. Like I'm someone's pet. A muscle in my arm twitches. Panic sends a hand down to my belly button. Gotta dig it out!

Dixie holds my wrist in a vise-like grip, but tender concern flows from her eyes. "Et si elle cesse de les prendre?"

A bead of sweat rolls down Jazmine's forehead. "What if she stops taking them?"

Sadness flickers across the doctor's face. "Withdrawal is exceedingly painful and nearly always fatal. Better to euthanize her than put her through that."

Jazmine shakes her head at Dixie. "Cela la tuerait."

How will I survive even ninety days of emotional overload let alone five years? Might as well kill me now.

One arm around my shoulder, Dixie helps me down off the table. I stand barefoot on the cold tiles and stare at the floor. My legs wobble. Swollen teardrops splash on my feet. What was so wrong about wanting an accepting family?

Dixie pulls me tight against her. The woman rocks back and forth, like she's comforting some little kid. "Ça va bien se passer, ma chérie. Tu seras heureuse. Et nous trouverons un moyen de te garder plus longtemps."

Strange—her voice brings peace though I understand nothing of what she says.

The doctor hands Dixie a pamphlet—Getting the Most Out of Your Sex Toy, no doubt. "Let her rest until morning," she says. "Tomorrow, spend as much time as possible intimate with her. And for the next two weeks, keep her isolated from everyone else. That's crucial."

Dixie brushes a fingertip down my cheek, wiping away the trail a tear left. "Allons, ma chérie. On va rentrer à la maison."

Back in her room, the woman retrieves a box from the dresser and hands it to me. Inside's a cashmere robe—crazy soft—and a pair of ballet flats.

When Dixie kisses my cheek, my body throbs—the remnants of my previous dose—probably too soon for the implant to be taking effect. Too late as well. A tremor rocks me. The room spins. The heart burns against my chest. I throw out an arm to grab the bed post, but the moment passes, and the world returns to normal.

Dixie takes my hand and leads me down the long hallway, across the great room, and through the doors into the garden. Dark clouds scud low across the morning sky. Occasional drops of rain splash against my face. The damp wind penetrates to the bone. Dixie pulls off her coat and wraps it around me. I press against her for shelter. And warmth. I need the physical contact. Bad.

On the grass beyond the pool and the fountain a helicopter waits. The woman urges me on toward the aircraft, till Jazmine catches up and stops us. She hands the coat back to Dixie. Then she gives me a quick hug before brushing a fingertip across the flower on my cheek. "I'll miss you, Stepanova. See you in ninety days."

Jazmine spreads my robe. Like that first day. But with everyone in the world watching now.

Her fingers wander lower, to find that little bit of Steri-Strip. With her hand on my waist, Jazmine's eyes search mine. A few days ago, her touch ignited passion and a desperate need. Somehow, they've passed my body to Dixie.

The girl kneels long enough to remove my ankle bracelet. When she stands again, she smiles like I'm her long-lost sister come home again. Jazmine slides her arms around my bare waist and presses her lips against mine—a lover saying a tender goodbye. Afterward, her eyes still glow.

"Yesterday, the court approved your adoption," she says. "And a name change. Farewell, Anastasie Bijou Dubois." With that, she strides off toward the manor.

Wait! I take a single step after her. "What about Anya? You can't take away my name!" All the girl does is wave at me.

At Dixie's urging I wrap her coat around me again and take a seat in the back of the helicopter. The blades spin up, and soon enough, we're airborne. I close my eyes and pretend that I'm with Brit on the way to her house after soccer.

Twenty minutes later, we land on the grass next to a runway at a small airport. Dixie leads me into a nearby hangar that seems deserted, except for a twin-engine private jet. As soon as we're aboard, one of the crew secures the door.

Dixie waves me toward a leather-upholstered seat. I snuggle into its plush cushions and close my eyes. A moment later, the woman spreads her coat over me.

Takeoff proves uneventful. With all of the shades drawn, I can't even guess our flight path. Does it matter? With my expiration date so near, escape would be pointless.

Hours later, we land. The aircraft taxis to a stop in front of a huge hangar, and one of the crew opens the hatch. This time, Dixie leads me a short distance to another helicopter. And yet another leather seat.

I curl up as tight as physics will allow. My need for Dixie's touch —to quiet the madness—has become desperate. Without her urging, I dare not let my hand find bare flesh. But I moan like a toddler in pain. One leg twitches. A tremor runs the length of the other. My arms convulse when vertigo spins my world. Bile rises in my throat. I open my mouth and breathe deep of the chill air.

Dixie leans close, slips a hand through the front of my robe, and brushes warm fingertips down my abdomen. "C'est dommage, ma chérie. La Dr. Campbell a dit que tu iras mieux demain matin." With her touch, the tension in my muscles bleeds away.

Only the faint whine of turbines disturbs the silence as we fly north over small islands, pine trees, and clouds reflected in blue water. Another round of tremors—though milder than before— passes through me. I close my eyes and press my face against Dixie's shoulder till the nausea fades.

When I feel better, I gaze out the window again. Pastel colors streak down from the heavens. Northern lights paint the sky. Or another side effect of the drugs.

Eventually, we fly over a large estate—the first visible habitation in an hour—before turning and starting our descent.

Mansion doesn't quite describe the house or the grounds. Ruins of a castle, maybe. Thousands of acres of parkland surround a stone building that would take weeks to explore. It figures, I guess. She's got the bread to buy a human sex toy and probably the influence to get away with it. Anyhow, nobody's gonna travel all the way to northern Canada to look for some runaway kid from Pennsylvania.

We land close to a newer addition—a massive iron and glass structure connected to the main building. The crew opens the door, but Dixie holds her palm out toward me. "Attends ici."

So I wait as people file out of an old set of wooden doors and form a line in front of the stone wall. Dixie stands like an empress before them, hands clasped behind her back. "J'ai adoptée la fille de ma défunte cousine." She motions for me, so I stumble down the steps and walk across the grass. The woman has me stand in front of her. "Elle s'appelle Anastasie Bijou Dubois."

Yeah. I remember the je m'appelle thing from French class. I wobble into a curtsy and promptly lose my balance. Dixie's strong arms rescue me. Her touch stills my trembling muscles. She kisses my cheek and then draws me close by her side. "La jeune fille est fragile, je ne veux pas qu'elle erre dans la maison. Veillez à ce qu'elle reste dans ses appartements."

Among the women and children assembled in front of us stands a girl my height with strawberry blonde hair in a long braid and a seriously cute freckled face. My heart stutters. I return her grin. Pointless to be thinking of girls at all, but I don't have many opportunities for friendship.

Dixie runs the fingers of one hand through my red hair. "Je veux qu'elle apprenne le français, alors, ne parlez pas anglais avec elle. De plus, elle possède une imagination débordante, alors ne croyez pas tout ce qu'elle dit."

She presses a hand against my back side and nudges me toward the door. Some of the children scamper away across the grass. The rest of the crowd follows us inside and disperses. Except the strawberry blonde girl, who lingers till Dixie hugs her. The kid extends a hand toward me, emerald eyes gleaming. "Je suis son petite-fils. Je m'appelle Courtenay. Bienvenue."

If the girl wore a little makeup and something more figure-flat-tering than a bulky cashmere sweater, she'd be awesome pretty.

In my mental haze, I struggle to remember any French. "Enchantée," finally comes to mind. I hold the girl's hand longer than is polite. Way longer. Red touches her fair skin, but the girl's emerald eyes never leave mine

At least till Dixie urges us to follow. "Suis moi! Courtenay, toi aussi," the woman hangs a right at the first intersection, then strides down a long hallway, past oil paintings of women, and a few life-sized statues. Overhead—three stories up—the evening sun shines through narrow windows.

The massive oak doors in front of us open as we approach. Beyond them, the hallway stretches on into the distance—beneath ancient stone archways—till obscured by a green haze.

Moss covers parts of the floor. In a few places, flowering vines cling to the walls, their sweet fragrance hanging in the air. Farther along, water drips down the rock. A hummingbird darts from a blos-som to Dixie's outstretched hand, and then disappears back down the hallway.

A muscle in my leg cramps. I lean against the wall to keep from falling. Dixie says something in French—almost a whisper—and Courtenay rushes to my side. The woman eyes us for a moment before walking back to me and holding me in her arms.

The storm dissipates. For now. My body won't last much longer, though. With Dixie holding my hand, we continue our journey. The three of us pass another archway, this one covered with moss. To our right, an open doorway leads outside. No. Not outside. When we step through, my eyes rise from the garden, up past the towering oaks. High overhead, steel girders and glass form a sparkling canopy.

Massive trees and a meadow spread out before us. Sunshine warms my face. A cobblestone walkway wanders out past the oaks. Off to one side, water splashes down a rock wall into a pool.

For a moment, wonder disperses the shadows. I draw clean air deep into my lungs and stretch my arms above my head. Five to seven years remain. How soon will this beautiful place become my tomb?

Dixie swirls around, arms out, skirt flying. Her smile turns innocent for once. "Ici, c'est notre aire de jeux."

My heart stutters. Not at seeing an old woman acting like a child. Not at the ethereal beauty surrounding us. But at the realization that this Dixie isn't the woman who groped me beside the pool. That Dixie would have danced like a ballerina in this enchanted place. Not like a drunken penguin. What happened?

Courtenay performs cartwheels across the grass—definitely a wild child—then parks on a nearby bench and pats her hand against the seat next to her. "Assieds-toi."

Dixie answers her phone and wanders off, so I take my place beside Courtenay and wait. I'm still bouncing from the most recent dose. And the pellet doesn't seem to be working. At least not yet. Chills alternate with heat—I need Dixie to hold me. Now.

When the woman returns, she stops in front of Courtenay. "Il faut que je parte," she says. "Je la laisse à ta charge. Tu comprends?"

Fear and joy mingle on Courtenay's face. She dips her head. "Oui, Mémère."

With that, Dixie rushes off across the grass and disappears through the archway. She's gone. I'm dead if she doesn't hold me when the next wave hits. The air turns freezing cold. A drop of sweat rolls down my forehead. Muscles tense for the approaching tremors. I may die alone. Today.

Courtenay studies me with a worried frown. "Tu vas bien?"

My body shakes in response. "Any chance you speak English?"

She grabs my hand and urges me to my feet. "Let's go." The girl leads me out along the trail through the oak trees. A few minutes later, we arrive at a cottage. Down a short hallway lies a cozy bedroom with a window that looks out over a garden. I flop down on the bed and curl up tight.

Courtenay tugs at my clothing. "She said you need touch."

Too weak to resist, I yield my robe and roll over. A drop of moisture rolls down my cheek. Another burns my eye. I roll my head back. My breaths come in ragged spasms. Eyelids squeeze shut against the pain. Guess the new Dixie didn't read the owner's manual.

The bouncing subsides. For a time. Optimism fades, though, when a leg muscle twitches. The pellet isn't gonna kick in before the next wave. I feel it coming, like a thunderstorm on the horizon. I sure hope Dixie returns before it kills me.

Faded memories of the girl I once was float across my waking dreams. I lie naked on cotton sheets, pain and arousal coursing through my tormented body. Heat builds again—slow as molasses this time—and then breaks into such a chill that my whole body shakes from the cold.

A tender hand brushes wet hair from my forehead. Courtenay stands beside the bed in a robe the twin of mine. Compassion shines from the girl's eyes as she leans over me. "I promised Mémère that I'd care for you."

My body responds to her touch as though to a potent aphrodisiac. Her pale skin deepens to red. Lips tremble. She glances back toward the door and stares open-mouthed as tremors vibrate through me. Then she brushes a tentative hand down my arm.

Yeah. Whatever. Better hurry. I bury my face in a pillow, unable to bear the light any longer.

Sudden warmth presses against my side. Arms wrap tight around my waist and roll my body halfway on top of hers. My breasts press against the girl's side. Our legs intertwine. Her touch heals my fractured senses. Calms the raging whirlwind. My breathing slows. Beads of moisture drip down my cheek and splash against her shoulder.

One hand slides down my side and caresses my hip. The fingers of the other wander from my breasts down over my pubes. The girl might seem innocent enough, but someone taught her how to comfort a girl in pain. Ugh. Yeah. Dixie.

Clouds hide the sun. My eyelids flutter open to a vision of an angel face surrounded by a wild halo of ginger hair that fades to a strawberry blonde. Her emerald eyes shine perfect contentment deep into my soul. I'm hers now and forever.

The last of the tremors fade, leaving only peace. Too tired for anything else, I yield to unconsciousness. And dreams of an oriental landscape.

Chapter Twelve

Sunshine ripples in lazy arcs across the sheet in front of me. I yawn, stretch my arms, and press my face into the pillow. Warmth pulses through me, but there's no sense in getting out of bed while I'm feeling this good. At least not till the memories of that awful dream fade.

A grin creeps across my lips. Okay, so I wouldn't mind meeting that ginger-haired girl.

Bare feet pad across a wooden floor. My foster mom's gonna tell me to drag my tush out of bed and get ready for school. No doubt I'm late. I must not have set my alarm.

"Are you hungry?" The soft voice doesn't belong to my mother. Or Brit. Or her mom.

I'm well awake now, though. Jazmine—the drugs she gave me have finally left my system. Only to be replaced by something more subtle. And much deeper.

Fondness and a hint of terror flow from Courtenay's eyes. They gave her something as well. Nobody falls this far in love so fast on their own. I swing my legs over the side of the bed, stand, and slide my arms around the girl. Yeah. I'm hooked so bad I can't even convince myself it's really the drugs that love her. That need her.

"Are you hungry?" she says again.

Food. "Yeah." Bouncing leaves me without an appetite, though. At least for a while. But I need to eat. So I follow my new crush to the kitchen, where a picnic basket waits on the table.

A glance around the room convinces me we'll never cook our own food here. Yeah, there's a stove, but it's one of those ancient potbelly cast iron things that burns coal or wood. There's no fridge. Not any electricity. Just a couple of wall-mounted oil lamps. That's it. "Dixie sent breakfast?"

Courtenay bobs her head. "I went to the kitchen this morning. Mémère wants you to stay here, but I can get you American food, if you like." Her gaze wanders away from me for a few seconds before returning. "Mémère wants you to learn the French words for things, so I'll teach you."

Yeah. Right. "Not this morning. Okay? I'm still not completely with it." I may never be.

Courtenay nods. Then she opens the basket and sets containers of scrambled eggs, sausages, top-knot rolls, and jam on the table. The aromas wake up my stomach enough to eat a fairly normal breakfast. The rolls are actually pretty good with the raspberry jam.

After breakfast, Courtenay packs everything into the basket again. She takes my hand and leads me back along the trail to the ruins. We rest on a moss-covered bench. Well, I do. She paces. I haven't fully recovered from the bouncing yet.

To our left, stone archways cover a cobblestone trail. They stretch for the length of a soccer field, ending in massive wooden doors. Yeah. We came that way. To our right the pathway meanders around fallen stones and broken arches.

Courtenay sets the picnic basket on the grass at the side of the trail. "I'll take it back later," she says. Then the girl hugs me. "I am so glad you're here. I hate being alone. Mind if I show you your new home?"

"Why not?" So I take the hand she offers and walk beside her down the cobblestone pathway. I can deal with this. But sometime, Dixie's gonna want to play, and me loving Courtenay will only make things worse.

After fifteen minutes or so we arrive at a clearing. The girl leads me to a boulder. Granite, maybe. She sits on the thing and pats the rock beside her. "Assieds-toi." she says. Yeah. French. And she expects me to learn it. Fine. "Is Mémère Grandmother?"

The girl looks away again. Then back at me. "Oui," she says. She takes my hand and leads me farther along the cobblestone path.

Sunlight finds its way down to us, through glass and leaves and flowers. Its warmth brings a smile to my face. Yeah. I'm dying. I get that. But why let death ruin what remains of my life? I'm holding hands with a pretty girl—a new friend—catching some rays as we continue our nature trail thing.

Though I've never wandered the ruins of a stone mansion, the place seems familiar. Not déjà vu so much as the feeling you get when you've walked the same path a hundred times without paying attention. Then, one day, you notice things you never did before. Like one of the fallen arches that lies just so. Or the way moss grows on the side of a giant boulder. Or a bent tree that reaches its limbs toward the ground.

A tremor shakes my soul as we round a bend. I stop and stare with my mouth open. Courtenay—still smiling—halts. "What?"

"I know this place," I say. "The walnut trees. These stones. The way the pollen dances in the sunbeams." I sit down on a boulder—probably once a part of an arch—and press both hands to my head. Are the drugs doing this to me? I grew up in Erie, Pennsylvania. Not in the ruins of a castle on some island in the great white north.

Courtenay perches next to me and slides a hand along my waist to my back. Comfort flows from her touch. The shadows fade. I lean my head against her shoulder and close my eyes. I can't know what lies beyond the grove of walnut trees. Yet I do. I'm certain of it.

With a sigh, I push myself up off the rock and wander down the trail. Yes. Cherry trees. Pink blossoms. White across the tops. I find another boulder and run my fingers along its surface. I waited here for my mother. Here. Not Mamochka, though. Someone else. She never came.

I sit on the boulder, press both hands to my head, and close my eyes. Courtenay pulls me close. Her hands warm my back. And my soul. She calms the storm. But for how long? "You were here before, weren't you?" she says.

I shake my head. "I don't think so. But I do know this place."

The girl eases away from me. "Maybe you know her, then."

"Who?"

She leads me past the cherry trees and off to one side. The girl stops in front of a statue of a woman holding a doll. A plaque says

Iseabail Gilyova. The face belongs to my mother. Not Mamochka. She wears a heart identical to mine.

The doll triggers strange memories of a time I had white hair and large pink eyes. Yeah. Me. Somehow, I don't think that was in Erie.

"You were here," Courtenay says again. "Before me."

I pull the girl close. 'Cause I need her. Minutes pass. Finally, I step back and shake my head. "I don't know."

"I've spent most of my life at Dixie's," Courtenay says, "but the statue was here when they brought me to this place." Sadness clouds her pretty eyes. "We can ask Giselle. She's the one who found me in Scotland."

"Yeah. Maybe." But what's she gonna say? Iseabail was my mother? I grew up here?

Courtenay holds out a hand again. I take it and follow her to a sunny clearing. She lies down on a patch of moss. Comfy soft, it is. I snuggle close beside her and stare at the blue sky, glass, and steel girders above us.

Till my stomach rumbles. And Courtenay laughs. We walk back toward the old oak doors so the girl can go inside and find us something to eat.

Chapter Thirteen

Time passes strange here. Days. Weeks. Courtenay doesn't know the date. Giselle won't say. So I float in a dream, eyes closed, impatiently waiting for a certain ginger-haired girl to return.

The door to our cottage squeaks. I jump out of bed and rush to the kitchen, but it's only one of Dixie's staff leaving a picnic basket on the table. The woman nods a good morning and leaves, pulling the door closed after her.

I promised Courtenay I'd sleep in our bed instead of waiting outside the old oak doors. Like I did the last time she spent the night inside. With Dixie. The girl insisted that she'd be okay. Yeah. But her eyes said otherwise. And I couldn't help her.

I stayed home. For Courtenay. But the sleeping in our bed part of my promise proved difficult. I love the girl. Okay? But she's afraid of me rejecting her. Because of what Dixie's been doing to her since Giselle brought the girl here. I shake my head and open the basket.

Meatloaf and potatoes—my stomach growls at the scent of a hot meal. So I eat. Not that I'm hungry. But I'll need the energy. I didn't sleep very well. Old dreams pursued me through much of the night. To ever have peace, I need to find out what lies beyond the edge of my watercolor landscapes.

My hand goes up to my throat, but Mamochka's heart isn't there. Days ago, it broke loose and fell—who knows where? The thing is gone, and a part of my soul with it. Courtenay helped me search, but we found not a trace of the heirloom.

Back at Brit's house in New Brighton, I painted landscapes and portraits. I never had the courage to sketch the ocean that also troubled my sleep, though the sea's beauty surpasses that of the cherry grove.

Somewhere beyond the trees—at least in some of my dreams—a shattered wooden boat washed ashore on a sandy beach. Blood pooled in the bottom. My heart beats faster even now, remembering the anguish of those visions. I need to know what happened.

So I finish eating, step outside, and follow the cobblestone trail. The air grows thick around me. Not asthma. Pure terror. Not from Kyrill's abuse, but something worse. Is that possible? Muscles tense, but I walk on. To face my past.

Something happened out on the ocean. Or down on the beach. Tears cloud my vision, but I squeeze my eyes shut against the emotions. The memories I push away as well. I grew up in Erie. In the city. Not even close to cherry trees.

Mamochka took me south to get away from an abusive father. When I was almost fourteen, Papa found us. He killed my mother, and I was put into foster care in Beaver County. Not anywhere near the ocean. Yet my broken memory insists otherwise.

Why do I care so much what lies at the end of some stupid cobblestone trail? I stop for a moment. Even turn back for a few steps. But if I don't explore now, I may never know.

My shoulders rise in surrender. I close my eyes and lean my head against a stone archway. My life's a fantasy. It has to be. Or maybe I'm insane. I'm not here. I can't be. My fists clench against the call of the void—the urge to end it all. To walk out into the sea and never return. Right. The sea. In Beaver County, Pennsylvania. Not gonna happen.

As I wander through the cherry trees, a drop of rain hits my cheek. No doubt condensation dripping from the metal and glass ceiling above me. Another drop splashes against my face. The sea breeze greets me with its cold dampness. It buffets my kilt. Water drips from my ginger locks. I inhale deep of the salt air. Yes. Beyond the cherry grove, the ocean abides in all of its glory. It reaches to the horizon. In the distance, a thunderstorm flickers.

Before me—and a hundred feet below—lies the ocean, its waves pounding the rocky shore. "Jump," whispers l'appel du vide. "Be at rest." The void tugs at the emptiness in my soul. I lean into the wind and shiver at the darkness seeping from my heart. Rain falls in earnest now. Drops stream down my face. I brush the hair away from my eyes.

"Brit!" I scream her name into the approaching storm. As much as I love Courtenay and want to help the girl, it's my bestie that I miss. How could I have gotten so far away from her?

"Maman?" The small voice behind me doesn't belong to my bestie. Or to anyone else I know. I turn in slow motion as my heart pounds frantic in my temples. A timid young girl with bright pink eyes and crazy white hair stands just out of reach. A moment passes before I realize how tiny she is. And how frightened. Yeah. Like me as a toddler facing an angry Kyrill.

Several yards behind the little one stand two young women and two girls. The tallest—a redhead—eyes me with love and a touch of uncertainty. The other one. Yeah. The blonde. She could be me. The petite me. Except that she's nursing a baby. And digging it. The woman's braid hangs down past her waist. Her smile beams reassurance.

"Ruadh Maman?" The white-haired girl in front of me holds out a shaking hand. Terror fills her eyes. "I sorry," she says. "I taked. I give back you."

Am I that scary to her? The girl's leg twitches. Her eyes plead with me to please not hurt her. Not kill her family. Why me? I'm no threat. I sit on the ground in front of the kid, hoping to calm her fears. "It's okay," I say. After a moment, I hold out my hand.

Into my palm, she drops a glowing heart on a chain. The tension around her eyes melts. The girl turns and runs back to the blonde. "Okay now, Maman? I give back."

The blonde says something comforting to the child. The little one scrambles up her mother's side and digs beneath her blouse. The woman smiles at me as the others start back down the cobblestone trail. Her free hand rises. A fingertip brushes against something at her throat. Yeah. Without any doubt, the heart her mother gave her. She nods and walks away.

I watch till the group passes out of sight. Till the rain stops. And the sea mist disappears. Till there's a roof of glass and steel above me again. I glance back toward the ocean. Though l'appel du vide still beckons, an ancient stone wall marks the end of the cobble-stone pathway and of my watercolor landscape. A sigh lifts my shoulders. I'm living in a fantasy world.

Yeah. Okay. So maybe one more shell of the nesting dolls is open now. But another, smaller one remains. And I don't know much more than I did before. Except perhaps that life's more complicated than my watercolor dreams.

I open my hand to examine what I already know has to be there. A chain and a silver heart with a blue cross of St. Andrew. It's bright and almost hot enough to burn. As my heart pounds on in the silence, I turn the thing over. Yeah. Nì mi sìth—I'll make peace—a play on the motto of my Kirkpatrick ancestors. Heat flows from the metal down into my soul. The heart Mamochka gave me. In perfect condition. Why not? Isn't that how drug-induced magic works?

I latch the necklace around my throat and drop the heart beneath my sweater. Somewhere in the distance, the old oak doors squeal open. I run along the trail, hoping to find Courtenay. And what little remains of my sanity. I scream her name with every bit of my energy. A muffled reply echoes down the trail. She's back.

We meet near the boulder, at the edge of the cherry grove. We dance a crazy hug—round and round. Courtenay and I hold each other till our breathing slows. Till our hearts stop pounding. Till I can feast my eyes on her smiling face.

"That's my last time with Dixie," she says, though her eyes insist there's also bad news. "She promised me that we could bond soon."

My face morphs into a glowing smile. "I think we already have."

Her mouth forms a small circle. Then she laughs and shakes her head. "No. I mean the way Daoine Sìth mate. I want you and me to share our lives together." The joy in her eyes fades. Fear grows there. Does the girl actually think I'd reject her? Ever?

I pull her close again. The drugs they're giving me will result in my death in a few years. Or I'm insane. But yes, either way, I want to spend what remains of my life or my sanity with Courtenay. I press my face close to her ear. "It's you and me forever," I say.

After a few minutes, she eases away from my grasp. A wave of pain crosses her face. "One more night with Dixie, and we're free— the two of us."

"You said it was your last time with her."

Her smile fades to a worried frown. "Mine. Yes. I'm sorry, but you have one more."

One more. My head swings back and forth in denial. Even with the drugs, there's no way I'd forget that.

Sorrow grows on the girl's face. "You don't remember?"

I shake my head again. "No. How many times?"

"With this one, three."

"And she'll be mad at me, if I refuse." Yes. I see the truth of that in Courtenay's eyes. Dixie might torture us both. Perhaps even decide that she no longer needs either of us alive.

Chimes drift through the air. My heart stops. I hug Courtenay and start walking back toward the old oak doors. As I draw near, I remember Mrs. Wilkinson. What would she think of me surrender- ing rather than dying? An image flashes by. Her and my bestie crying for me. 'Cause I disappeared. Yeah. She'd be glad I'm alive.

As the old oak doors creak open, I hug Courtenay one last time. "I'll be fine," I say, hoping that's not a lie. Then I follow Dixie back down that long hallway to her quarters.

Chapter Fourteen

Weeks have passed—I'm not sure how many—since Dixie brought me here to be with Courtenay. I squeeze the girl's hand. We're never apart. And the love we share—whether drug-induced or not—continues to grow.

Courtenay wants to bond. Yeah. The girl blushes whenever she talks about it. Like we weren't naked together that first night. And I spent two weeks with Jazmine making porn videos. Okay, so I know my body's had sex. I just don't remember any of it. The drugs, you know. Not that I mind missing those particular memories.

Courtenay says you become bondmates by kissing. So we haven't done that. Not yet. The girl says it's not required, but there's usually a ceremony first. Yeah. I get that. Taking vows before God and witnesses. But we're prisoners. I don't think Dixie's gonna officiate at a wedding.

The woman's shoes click against the stone floor as she approaches. She's wearing an embroidered caftan. Gorgeous. She steps through the doorway and nods. "Bonjour, mes filles," she says. "C'est rougissant aujourd'hui, non?"

When I notice the long curved blade she's holding, I take a step backwards. For an instant, my father stands there. "He'll find you," the voices whisper. "He'll hurt you again."

"It's okay," Courtenay whispers from behind me. "Rougissant. Ruadhaich in Gaelic. It's a ceremony where one of your parents cuts off your braid so you can give it to the one you love as a promise that you'll bond with them."

The girl's eyes hold a deep affection. And fear of rejection. Even now. Not just from the drugs. I understand that. Would I spend the few years I have left with her? Of course. "What happens when we, um, bond?"

The girl's face turns a darker shade of red. Seconds pass while her eyes avoid mine. Finally, she says, "Chlann. Children. Family."

Marriage. Kids. Courtenay and me. I turned sixteen a few days ago—maybe a few weeks. I probably won't survive past twenty-one.

Courtenay doesn't care at all about pronouns, but she insists that being ruadh makes us boys. Both of us. Right. No way her body's male enough to get me pregnant, though. Unless Dixie's planning on artificial insemination, children ain't gonna happen.

What would Mrs. Andrews think? She never said Brit couldn't get married. And I'm not ashamed of loving someone who's not entirely male. A deep sigh lifts my shoulders. If this is what Dixie wants, I may not have a choice.

My desperate longing for family will never be satisfied any other way. Not with Mamochka gone. Not with the emotional scars from Kyrill's abuse. Not with my expiration date so soon. But Courtenay and I have each other. For now, at least. I may not have any future, but I'll embrace the present.

Courtenay tugs on my arm. Dixie's already well down the trail. We rush to catch up, and then follow the woman to the boulder near the statue of my mother.

I saw a movie once—human sacrifice involving a curved knife. On a large rock. I glance at Courtenay, but his face shows no fear.

Dixie motions for Courtenay to sit on the boulder. After saying something formal-sounding in French, the woman grabs hold of Courtenay's braid. She raises the knife and slashes through her hair, cutting it off close to the boy's head.

Kyrill! My scream echoes through the cherry trees. I run. Now as I did when the monster stabbed my mother. But I trip over a vine and plant my face in the dirt. Dixie catches up and pins me to the ground. Till Courtenay's close enough to hold me. Till my breathing slows. And the shaking stops.

I sit on the boulder and close my eyes while Courtenay braids my curly locks. The boy slides an arm around my waist, but I still flinch when Dixie pulls on my hair and the knife swishes close enough to shave my neck.

When the woman is finished, and I hold the short stub of my hair that passes for a braid, Courtenay urges me to stand. We hug.

He kisses me on the forehead. Then—with eyes that still fear rejection—he holds out his braid.

How could the girl think I'd refuse her? Sorry. Him. So I hold out mine and take his braid. Courtenay's smile warms my entire being.

Dixie sits on the boulder and motions for us to draw close. She slides the knife into a sheath. Then she opens a leather case and draws out a crystal bottle. She pours an amber fluid into three small glasses. To one she adds a few drops from a small vial.

The woman hands Courtenay and me a glass before raising her own. "Je vous souhaite tout le bonheur possible." She empties it in one swallow.

Courtenay grins at me, holds up her glass, and drinks it, though her lips twitch.

Me? My drink smells of vanilla. My eyes plead with Dixie. "I'm happy to bond with Courtenay. But I don't need this. Please?"

"Bois tout," she says and tips her glass up again.

Yeah. I don't need to know French to understand the woman. I don't get to remember my wedding night. But at least I'll have one. So I raise the glass and down it all. Then Courtenay and I follow Dixie back to the old oak doors.

Have you ever had a Frozen Russian? The feelings welling up in me are no surprise, but not any easier to ignore than previous times. As soon as Dixie leaves and the doors close, I grab Courtenay's hand and urge her back toward our cottage. Fifteen minutes, I figure, before I'm wasted.

A couple of women are leaving our small home as we arrive. They nod at us and chatter away in French. Courtenay turns red, but pulls me close before stepping into the house.

The table's set with a small feast. Roasted chicken. Potatoes. Various veggies. Even a bottle of wine. Like I need alcohol on top of the drugs. But I smile and nod when Courtenay pours me a glass.

The food tastes awesome, but Courtenay spends most of her time staring at me. Not eating. So I set my fork down and walk around the table.

Courtenay stands. She steps close—closer than is her wont. Tension grows around her eyes. Her muscles tremble. Her smile grows hesitant.

The girl said that reds have a sort of mating ritual before bonding. Every ruadhan—every last redheaded elf believes they'll be the one who will become male after bonding. But some are apparently better at romance than others. So I smile, lean close, and run my fingertips down her cheek. Were it my choice—if one of us has to become male—sorry, Courtenay, but I'd have her be the one. I already miss being blonde and petite enough that I don't want to think about what would happen to my brain if I grew facial hair.

After Courtenay finishes her wine, she sets down the glass. Something in the girl's eyes changes. Like her testosterone is kicking in. She moves close and brushes her lips against mine. Then she closes her eyes and kisses me like no one else ever.

Cinnamon warmth spreads across my mouth and down my throat. Blue shadows flicker in the evening. We part for breath, but my need for Courtenay overwhelms my emotions. Tears flow, though sadness and pain flee. We kiss again. Cinnamon—hot and sweet—flows through me. Warmth grows in my chest. My heart beats a crazy rhythm.

The girl leads me to the bedroom. All fear has departed from her face. No chance at all that I'll reject her. She seems to know better now. So we lie down—side by side—and kiss again. Till cinnamon and blue fire warm my entire being.

Courtenay's eyelids droop then. Muscles relax. Only her angelic smile remains. So I rest my head on her shoulder and surrender to the night.

Chapter Fifteen

His lips taste of honey and hot cinnamon, the sweetness of our kiss exploding in hunger across my soul. After the firestorm, only warm contentment remains. A gentle hand caresses my side. He nuzzles my ear and whispers "Cèol mo chridhe."

My sleepy eyes open to moonlight, blue and pure. My arms still tight about my lover's waist, I dare not move. Nor risk a shallow breath. Why would he want me? Even the fair-haired imagination of my dreams has to have some standards. What real boy would accept a girl with madness between her legs and tiny breasts?

My redhead has drifted off to sleep again. Angel face, hair floating in a cloud of spun copper, full lips relaxed in an easy smile—my beautiful lover could be a girl but for his flat chest. Is that the secret desire of my heart? An intersex girl like me? A feminine boy?

Well he is cute. My hand brushes his smooth cheek, leaving a trail of soft blue sparks. Cinnamon tickles my senses again in the dim glow. The air itself breathes thick and heavy with desire. I pull my shaking hand away from what has to be an illusion.

The boy seems so real. Disappointment shadows my joy. Only in a madman's dream would someone ever love me so freely.

Ghosts of troubled memories wander across the ceiling. Drugs. Sex. Bouncing. A little girl at a party. My dead body, face down in a swimming pool. But reflections of a long kiss in the night chase them all away, and draw me back toward the light.

Not ready to greet the morning, I yawn, stretch, and roll over. The girl—it has to be—lying next to me in a filmy cashmere nightgown—exudes tranquility. The low sound of her breathing assures me that she's still asleep. How can the girl be so much at peace, lying next to a stranger, someone she must know is a freak?

Was that passion ours? I never kissed anyone before. Not like that, anyhow. But afterimages of hope drift across my loneliness.

Who is this girl that she cares so much for me? I press my face into her hair—soft as cashmere and smelling of apples and mint. How did I end up in bed with her?

I sink back down and gaze at the ceiling. Hewn beams run between rough-plastered walls. Stone frames the single small window. The fireplace across the room glows a dull cherry red. A table with an oil lamp stands in one corner, next to a wooden rocker. Ramskins lie on the smooth plank flooring.

A cabin in the mountains? An old hunting lodge? This ain't Beaver Falls. Curiosity pushes me out of bed. I sway for a moment, one hand on the bedpost, till the world stops spinning, and I can breathe again. Drugs—a voice in my head whispers.

Beyond the door, I find a larger room with food still spread out on a dining table. Early morning reds and blues flood in through the windows. An old stone fireplace graces one wall. Ancient kitchen cabinets line another. I creep to the front door and peer out into the chill air. Somewhere in the east, the sun has already risen. High above, metal beams and glass partition the sky. To the west lies a stone wall—perhaps part of an old ruin. My heart thumps double-time. I close my eyes and swear under my breath. This place is nowhere near my foster home.

Jazmine—the voice in my head whispers. Then Dixie. I return to the bedroom and plop down beside the girl. "Wake up," I whisper, an insistent hiss.

The body next to me groans a soft, "Oui, Mémère." Sleepy green eyes dominate the innocent elfin face of my dreams. After the moment it takes them to focus, her wide eyes explode with joy. She inhales—a quiet squeal. "You're awake!"

"Well, yeah. I do that sometimes."

Her lilting Scottish brogue strikes me right away, but it isn't until she sits up that I remember her flat chest. Well, not completely flat. But—yeah—is this the fae boy of my dreams?

Eyes still wide, he places a hand on mine. His gentle touch ignites a desperate attraction—something beyond what Jazmine's drugs ever induced. I snatch my hand away, but the loss is too great for sanity to bear. So I take his hand, lean forward, and press my lips against his. Cinnamon fire erupts in a wild frenzy.

What is wrong with me? My body jerks upright. I'm not even sure what sex my lover is. My eyes dart toward the door. Something inside screams at me to flee before it's too late.

Tenderness shines from the boy's face. "It's okay. I'm Courtenay, your bondmate. Mémère told me you might be confused in the morning." She—yeah, the voice is that of a girl—she runs fingertips across my cheek. Soft blue sparks rain down in the dim light. Love shines from her eyes.

I stare at the girl's fingers, thinking about some of the horror movies I've seen. What planet is she from? How soon do I die? "Where are we?" I say it aloud, but already know the answer. In a faded memory, I stand beside a swimming pool while an older woman explores my body with her hands. "Dixie," I say.

The girl nods. "Oui. Mémère."

Memory strikes me so hard I wince from the pain. A police officer lying on the ground, smoke rising from his dead body. Another cop with his gun raised. Pushing away the terror, I try to joke about my situation. "So, do you kiss all of the girls that Dixie buys?"

Courtenay flinches as though I slapped her, then shakes her head. "I'm sorry, Anastasie. Truly I am. Dixie told me that if we didn't bond, you'd die. And I do love you."

Nobody will miss me when I'm dead. Loneliness wraps around my chest, cutting off life and breath. My hand seeks hers. "Forgive me," I say. As we touch, my need for a friend overwhelms everything else, sending a cascade of blue lightning tumbling from my fingers to hers. As I gape, the feeling passes and the torrent diminishes. "What the—" I whisper, not meaning to say it aloud.

A thoughtful smile and a trace of pity replace the pain on the girl's face. "The áed you see is a form of dealan—electrical energy." Her fingertips leave trails of blue stars across the back of my hand. "The fire of our love." Her lips brushing across mine prod my heart. She leans back and smiles. "It comes to reds who have bonded. It started with our first kiss and brings the change that will make one of us male and the other female."

Chapter Sixteen

Courtenay nuzzles me awake before the dawn, while the shadows of night still reign, and moonbeams dance across our glass ceiling. Pink and violet hues rise in the east. Morning will soon light the countryside.

The best sleep is always the last little bit of coasting before I get up. I stretch, yawn, and roll away from Courtenay's warmth. With my eyes closed, I see our bond—a trail of silver and gold sparkles that hangs in the air between us. In the week since we first kissed, it's grown strong.

I don't get it. Okay? These things don't happen to humans. Not even intersex ones. So it must all be from the drugs. Hallucinations, ya know? My shoulders roll up in a careless shrug. At least I'm alive and sharing my insanity with someone I love.

Courtenay tickles me—blue sparks floating from her fingertips —till I beg her to stop. Her grin heals much of what ails me. Nobody ever smiled that way for me before. Except Brit. Yeah. Brit.

"I knew I'd be the male," Courtenay says, pulling up her night-gown. Sex and gender aren't the same thing. I get that. They don't have to match. But I don't see any physical changes. The girl still looks the same between her legs. On the female end of intersex. And her personality hasn't changed.

The girl rolls her eyes. Like I'm missing something obvious. She taps on the faint purple line that runs down her abdomen. Even that was there before. "Cnapan leanaibh," she says and touches several tiny blue lumps gathered right where the scar ends.

She shakes her head again, closes her eyes for a moment, and then says, "Baby bumps." Tenderness carries her certainty across the bond and deep into my soul. She's trying to share one of the most joyful moments of her life with me.

I smile and nod. "Babies," I say. Not because I believe her. Because I love the girl, and I'm desperate that not just one of us be crazy.

"You're female, then," she says, suddenly timid. Her eyes widen. Wonder flows across the bond. Since I no longer have any idea how sex is defined for elves, I pull up my nightgown.

Courtenay points at her scar. "Brù," she says. She tugs at my hand, so I run a fingertip down her abdomen. Gotta admit the purple thing feels like it's thicker now than it was before. More prominent. Something. It runs from just under her bellybutton all the way down to her pubes. At that end, it disappears down into her belly.

The girl touches my abdomen with a fingertip. Yeah. I have a scar there, too. So I guess we're both male. Except that the line down my middle has faded so much that I'm not sure whether it's there anymore.

I meet Courtenay's eyes. "I love you," I say. Because fear and uncertainty are going out from me across the bond. She smiles and nods. There's something else so obvious that she doesn't want to say it. She sends mild amusement with her love.

D'oh! My hands flash up to my breasts, which are at least a cup size larger than they were a week ago. Is that what makes me female? Boobs? That and a faded brù line?

Okay. I see it now. Déjà vu hits. The girl under the cherry trees. Males bear children. Females nurse them and heal them. I send my love across the bond. "Sorry for thinking you were a girl," I say.

"I was," she says. "Years ago." Courtenay retrieves her braid from the shelf where I keep it. She points at the white tip. "White locks, pink eyes—on her mother's breast she lies." She slides her fingertip to the middle—a pale blonde. "Blue eyes, golden braid—gentle girl, at home she stayed." Finally, she touches the ginger end, where it was cut off. "Redhead running through the vale—soon enough he'll think he's male."

She returns her braid to the shelf. "We were both girls. We were both boys. Now, we're mother and father." To her it makes complete sense.

I try not to let my doubt escape across the bond, but insanity or drugs seem a more logical explanation for my situation than my being an elf. Okay, Daoine-Sìth—a Fair Folk child. Yeah, and I was hiding out among the humans for what reason?

Courtenay sits beside me on the mattress again. This time her eyes find mine and hold them fast with her love. "The Outsider humans who took care of me were kind. They never tried to deny what I was. They never shamed me for being different. They protected me from the bullies and from the doctors who wanted to make me look more human." She slides in close. "But, after my parents died, I never saw one of my own people again. Until you came here."

A single tear runs down the girl's cheek. I pull her tight. Yeah. I'm gonna have to find a way to hold her that doesn't mean being overwhelmed by cinnamon and blue sparks. Right?

Chapter Seventeen

Chills drag me back to consciousness—another Arctic wave break-ing over my body. Jazmine said the implant was milder than the earlier drugs. And lasted three months. Maybe so, but I'm already bouncing, and harder than before. Dixie needs to send me back for repairs before my warranty expires.

Courtenay slides her arms around me and pulls me close. Empathy flows across the bond, easing my tension, spreading peace and comfort through weary muscles. For a time. All too soon, cold becomes scorching heat. And the tremors start again.

I'm well into my fourth crash and burn cycle when a shadow passes overhead—a helicopter. A short while later, the chimes start —our call to meet Dixie. Except that I can't walk. Not with my muscles knotted so tight.

Tenderness and fear war across my bondmate's face as she considers helping me stand. Like that is even possible. Finally, she shakes her head and rushes out of the room. I close my eyes and press my face into the pillow as boiling hot water covers my body.

Someone rolls me on my back. Giselle. So soon? Courtenay stands behind the woman. My bondmate smiles, but her lips twitch, and fear seeps across the bond. They pull me to my feet and ease me down into a wheelchair. Someone cries aloud—like a toddler in agony.

Courtenay squeezes my hand and sends her love through the bond. I open my eyes and smile for her, though echoes of pain overwhelm my senses. Muscles crawl and twist. I breathe through an open mouth, arch my back, and wait for death to take me home.

We land at the Stepanova estate in New York, though I don't remember the first helicopter ride or the long jet flight. As soon as the cockpit door opens, Jazmine's beside me, pressing something hard and cold against my bare leg. Pain spikes to madness. Then silent darkness drags me into the night.

I wake on a gurney. Courtenay smiles at me. Love and excitement dance across the bond. Though I'm exhausted, the sea is as calm as glass. Puffy white clouds float across a dark blue sky. Life has pushed death away. For a time.

Dr. Campbell checks my blood pressure and my pulse. She examines my eyes. She runs a fingertip across my cheek and shakes her head. The woman presses here and there around my abdomen. Eventually the muscles around her eyes relax. She nods at Jazmine and walks out of the room.

My bellybutton itches. One hand slides down to find a new Steri-Strip there. They replaced the implant. But it couldn't be working so soon—they must have given me something else. Something stronger. Certainly better. Hope the price of withdrawal isn't a cruel death.

Jazmine leans over me. Her hand wanders close—as if to stroke my cheek—but she doesn't touch me. I belong to Courtenay now and always—however brief my time with the girl may be. Jazmine sighs and then pushes the gurney down the hallway to the bedroom where she and I once stayed.

When the girl stops, I swing my legs off the side and sit up. With Courtenay's help, I stand. The bouncing's gone, but it's only my bondmate's dealan surging through the bond that keeps my swaying body upright.

And—yeah—Jazmine's holding my other arm. I turn to thank her. To say that I'll be fine. But I have to look up—the girl's at least four inches taller than when Dixie bought me. My eyes wander down to her feet—expecting heels—but the girl's wearing ballet flats. A tremor runs through me—not from any of the stupid drugs, either.

I take a deep breath and release it slowly, glance at Courtenay, and then shuffle across the room to the mirror.

The old Anya—the petite one—stands there, frowning at me. Her hair's a pale blonde. I move closer. Yes. My eyes are steel blue again. The faded ghost of an orchid tattoo graces her cheek. I turn my head toward Jazmine and wait till our eyes meet. Yeah. Like that. Then I ask her a question that should be obvious. "How tall am I?"

Jazmine eyes me the way Brit did whenever I asked her something that she thought was really obvious. Like I wasn't six inches taller three months ago. With red hair. And green eyes. With a vibrant watercolor tattoo on my cheek. The girl just shakes her head and leads me back toward the bed. "I should leave you two alone," she says and walks out of the room.

Courtenay sits beside me on the mattress and takes my hands in hers. I wait as contentment flows through me. The girl sighs. Once. Twice. Then smiles at me. "When Daoine-Sìth bond, one remains ruadh and the other returns to being òr. At least externally." She kisses my cheek with a hint of blue fire and cinnamon. "Ma chérie, je t'aime, telle que tu est." Affection flows across the bond, intense as the sunlight outside.

The girl lies back on the bed and tugs at my hand. She brushes my fingertips over her abdomen. One of the baby bumps has moved farther down her belly. And grown. Yeah. We're married, okay? I love Courtenay. But I don't inspect her body every day. And I've been kinda self-focused lately, with the bouncing and all. Anyhow, our baby's growing. Our baby. Hers and mine. Well, his and mine to an elf, I suppose.

I run gentle fingertips across the bump again, raining soft blue fire down on our child. Cinnamon tickles my nose. The smile on Courtenay's face becomes a grin. The baby's digging this—her joy pulses through my bondmate and across the bond.

I lie in Courtenay's arms for maybe an hour before Jazmine taps on the door and walks in. "You have a visitor," she says. Then she walks over to the closet, picks out a dark blue dress and hands it to me. "Stepan would like you to join him as soon as possible." As she's leaving, she throws a glance at Courtenay. "Alone."

Visitor. Dixie stayed behind. Stepan or Zinaida would have walked into the room. By now, nobody in Beaver County remembers me. Well, Brit and her mom might. But they're not here. So who?

Courtenay helps me with the dress. It's satin. Or maybe silk. Very nice. I pull the belt tight and walk out of the room.

With all of the things I've forgotten—or that have been erased—I remember well the long hallway and the great room where Stepan waits. Logs crackle and burn in the fireplace. Sun shines down through the skylights. Ceiling fans whisper their slow dance.

A man sits at the table with Stepan. Yellow letters run down his navy blue sleeve. US MARSHAL. Ilya Koshkin. Or someone like him. Come to claim me, no doubt. I glance back over my shoulder, hoping for a glimpse of Courtenay.

When Stepan smiles and nods at me, the marshal turns in his chair. No. Not Ilya Koshkin. I walk past the man and kiss Stepan on the cheek. "What can I do for you, Papa?" I say it as though no one else in the room matters. No way I'm leaving Courtenay. No matter what the cop says.

Stepan rises from his seat and hugs me. "I am so proud of you, Anastasie. So proud. Madame Dubois tells me that you've been a delight to her these past three months." With a smile and a hand gesture, he urges me to sit in a chair. The nice leather one beside him. Yeah. Away from the US marshal. Then he smiles at me again. "This is Ilya Koshkin. He says that you're his daughter."

Ilya Koshkin? Not even close. Unless the previous one was an impostor.

"Really? My father's in prison. Albion State, I think. His name's Kyrill Gilyov."

"No, Anya," the marshal says. "Please don't tell me that you're Praskovya, Anya's identical twin sister. We've been through that fantasy too many times already."

I lean back in my chair and raise an eyebrow at Stepan. "If the truth doesn't interest him, why is he here?"

"I came to take you home," the man says. His chest heaves in a sigh. "Again." He pulls a folder out of his briefcase and lies it open on the table, exposing a stack of papers. Familiar-looking ones. With a passport on top of them.

So I go through the documents—one at a time—explaining what they are. And what happened. Again. Praskovya and Anya swapped. Though surely this Ilya Koshkin already knows. "Take me home?" I say. "Seriously? I'm not your adopted daughter."

Determination fires the marshal's eyes. "Then prove it," he says. This time he pulls a laptop out of his briefcase. After plugging in a USB fingerprint reader, he brings up a browser window and goes to some official-looking website. "Here," he says, and pushes the fingerprint reader toward me.

I shake my head. I ain't that stupid. Brit could write an app that says Anya Koshkina whenever I put a hand close to a fingerprint gizmo. Even a fake one.

The US marshal—if he really is a cop—slides the reader toward Stepan. Papa scowls at the man, but brushes a fingertip across the sensor. A few seconds later, an arrest photo of him is there, along with his entire legal history. Everything. Stepan nods at me. Do it, his eyes say.

So I brush my fingertip across the little glass window. The browser asks me to swipe it again. So I do. And the screen says Praskovya Kyrillovna Gilyova. Dude! I raise an eyebrow at Stepan. Why would Beaver County report me missing if my case was legit transferred to Erie County? Papa just smiles and nods his head. I'm dismissed. I kiss him on the cheek, and then return to my room without a backward glance. But I can feel Ilya's angry brown eyes following me.

Courtenay hugs me and says we're leaving, so as soon as the US marshal's car is out the front gate, our pilot spins up the turbines. The helicopter takes the short hop to the airport, and we begin our long jet flight home. In my leather seat, I lie as close to Courtenay as possible. Then shut my eyes and retreat into unconsciousness.

Chapter Eighteen

Months pass in the quiet of our meadow. Days grow short. In the evening, the northern lights turn the glass canopy into a kaleidoscope of rainbow colors.

On a bright winter day, particles of dust sparkle across the sunbeams. High above—beyond the glass and steel ceiling of our prison—clouds prance across the afternoon sky. Like lambs dancing in the pasture on a day without rain.

Courtenay stops in front of a mound of silver-green moss. Its tendrils wave back and forth in the breeze. Except there isn't any breeze. Creepy. My bondmate grins at me before pulling off her cashmere sweater and kilt. Nude, she lies down on the moss. And sinks in.

The stuff moves, enclosing my love in its embrace. Courtenay sits up and grins at me. Like she's not at all in danger of being eaten by a plant. There's a reason you don't see any elves around, okay? I get that the animals all love me, but this is different. I don't fraternize with plants that can kill me.

Courtenay brushes a hand across the green carpet beside her. "She's almost here."

"Who?" Dixie? We see her once a month. Giselle, maybe twice.

"Taylor—our daughter." Amusement flows across the bond. You're not paying attention, it says.

"It's only been—what—six months?" But then I remember I live in a drug-induced fantasy where anything can happen. Or we're two elves in captivity, and this is all normal.

A careless shrug lifts my bondmate's shoulders. "The first birth for Daoine-Sìth usually takes six months."

"Today?"

"Now," she says.

"Right now?" My heart pumps like a wild racehorse. "You're sure it's a girl? Shouldn't we at least have a midwife?"

Courtenay sits up. She's going to lecture me. "Even a wee bànag knows that babies are all female," she says. "White locks, pink eyes—on her mother's breast she lies."

While my mouth is still open, the girl rolls back on her bed of moss and spreads her knees. One grunt from Courtenay and something slides out of her. Just like that. A doll. One of those with a head too large for its body. With big eyes and a cute little mouth. My gaze wanders back down the pathway toward the statue. Yeah. Exactly like the one Iseabail's holding.

I suck in my breath. Moss covers both Courtenay and our daughter. Soon enough, it withdraws, leaving a clean newborn and mother.

The doll—our daughter—is the cutest baby ever. No, really. Cuter than any anime character. She has large eyes. They're pink. But that's not being fair to the depth of their color. Or their beauty. And—yeah—she's got lots of white hair. Like polished silver, gleaming in the sun.

Our daughter struggles in Courtenay's arms. She trills. Or purrs, maybe. Like a human cat. My bondmate rolls to her feet and hands me our baby. Ours! Taylor presses her face against my chest and starts digging with her hands. Like a kitten. Yeah, I know what that means. So I pull up my sweater and help her find a breast.

An awesome feeling flows into me. One I recognize. An overwhelming need for physical touch satisfied—my baby against me. I smile at Courtenay and send my love across the bond. I'm not much more than sixteen. Not sure I'll survive till seventeen. But I'm the mother of an elfin baby. Me. Yeah. Happens all the time.

Dressed again, Courtenay slides an arm around my shoulder and kisses my cheek. We stroll off toward the cherry trees in a cinnamon haze. Our baby purrs when her face isn't pressed tight against my breast.

Puffy white clouds play tag above us. Butterflies dance among the flowers. A hummingbird flies close, hovers long enough to wink congratulations, and then moves on. After an hour under the trees, we wander back down the cobblestone pathway, in no particular hurry to get home.

Someone left a picnic lunch on the table in our cottage, so I lay Taylor on our bed and start unpacking the food. Baked potatoes. Haricot verts—yeah, I finally learned the French for green beans. How long have I been here? And meatloaf. Don't let anyone tell you that elves are vegan.

Courtenay sets out plates, silverware, and glasses. Perfect company. Good food.

When we're finished, my bondmate sits close beside me, but facing the other way. She keeps grinning and glancing at me. Her love and amusement flood across the bond.

Then she pulls her hair back and runs a fingertip up the front of her ear. To the point. Yeah. Like an elf might have. Guess males get those as well. Fine. I can accept that her ears are growing. And, actually, they look pretty cool.

My bondmate smiles at me. Like she always does when I'm missing something obvious. Love and compassion surge across the bond. She brushes the hair away from my ear and runs delicate fingertips up to the point of mine.

Terror seizes me. I jerk away from her touch. Away from the waterfall of soft blue sparks that fall from her fingers. Am I that afraid of being Daoine-Sìth? Of not being human? Is it so important that none of this be real?

My heart beats a frantic syncopation. I back away from Courtenay. I want to run away from this place and keep running. Till I'm back home with Brit and completely human again. Just a dumb blonde intersex girl. Yeah. That.

Except maybe I was never human. And I need Courtenay—desperately bad. I can't bear to hurt the girl again, either. So I hug her tight and let my tears flow. Till my gut spasms like I'm some little kid without any hope in a cruel, cruel world.

Courtenay? She just smiles, says, "Je t'aime," and holds me tight while our baby sleeps.

Chapter Nineteen

Courtenay jostles me awake while frost still clings to the glass above us, while the sky sends dark red beams down into the meadow. While the butterflies sleep. The girl says nothing at all, but grins and runs a hand down her abdomen.

"Can it wait till morning?" I ask, trying desperately to keep my eyes open. Tremors and thermal waves hit me yesterday at dusk and continued well into the night. Beside me, Taylor scowls. She didn't get much sleep either.

"Now," Courtenay says and tugs on my hand. Hard. A hint of terror clouds the excitement she sends across the bond. Then she sighs and gives me her teacher frown. "Even for Daoine-Sìth, child-birth can go astray. Quickly."

She stands and starts walking across the meadow. Almost running, actually. She stops under the archway leading to the main hallway—or whatever you want to call the cobblestone path that leads from the old oak doors out to the orchards.

Her eyes apologize now—if not her words. "I left Eilean nan Sìthean when I was a wee bànag. All I know is that the fathers always used a leabaidh breith when giving birth."

I nod to my bondmate—my love—my life. I take her hand and rush down the pathway. Taylor grips me tight and squeals—not sure whether that's joy or terror.

Courtenay spent most of her childhood in foster care with humans. She's so careful with me. How would I feel if I'd grown up with elves? Would I understand her better?

Far off in the distance—back toward the old oak doors—the chimes begin. Courtenay glances that way but doesn't slow down. Dixie will have to wait.

I've been bouncing for days, but I told Courtenay there was time enough for Remie to be born before we flew back to New York to get my new implant. There's no lying across the bond. Not possible. Courtenay knew I was well into withdrawal's second wave. But she just shook her head and agreed to wait.

As she strips in front of her moss bed, my bondmate does a little happy dance. Well, okay, so the girl looks like she needs to pee. She's that close to delivery. After Courtenay lies down on the moss, I run a hand down her abdomen. Five lumps remain visible—from pea size to baseball. The sixth one moved down into her uterus two weeks ago. The one that will crawl out today. Well, now, actually! Courtenay groans and leans back into the moss.

Seven babies over a two year period. Each three months apart. Seven! The thought alone wears me out. Heat washes over me—not quite scalding. Muscles tremble. Taylor squeals, runs up my side, and clings to one of my breasts. The pain subsides. A little. My daughter eyes me with concern, but starts feeding.

Courtenay rises from the bed and hands me our second baby. Daoine-Sìth childbirth. Just like that. Then she urges me back down the trail to the hallway that leads to the old oak doors. Another tremor reminds me that we need to hurry.

Remie quivers as she feeds for the first time. Remie. The Daoine-Sìth give their children a boy's first name and a girl's middle name. Dixie suggested we go with a single, gender-neutral one. Then she gave us a list of acceptable choices. Pick one for each baby, she said.

Dixie frowns at us. Fire burns in the woman's eyes. Till she sees that I'm breast-feeding two now. Then she nods and smiles and waves us on. "Remie," I say, though the woman doesn't ask.

A few minutes later, we meet Giselle in the manor hall. She says something to Dixie—in French, of course. After a brief conversation, Giselle turns to me. "I need your silver heart. I'll return it when you get back."

Dixie's scowl grows deep while I hesitate. My throat tightens. Breathing becomes difficult. But I sigh, unclasp my necklace, and hand it to Giselle. "Please," is all I manage to say.

Dixie waves us forward again. Through the doorway and into fresh snow. Across the courtyard to a waiting helicopter. Um, yeah, we're late.

Courtenay holds Taylor while I board and buckle myself in. Soon enough, she's strapped in beside me, and both of our daughters are under my sweater, tight against me. Sleeping, I would think, from the constant rumble of their purring.

The helicopter rises into a dark blue sky. Below us, snow and ice extend to the horizon in every direction. The morning sun burns an angry red low in the sky. I squeeze my bondmate's hand and close my eyes. Maybe it's only my babies transmitting their emotions to me, but life seems perfect right now.

Time slips past—as it always does on these trips—and soon enough, we're crossing a snow-covered walkway to a private jet in a hangar. One of the crew pops her head out of the hatch as we approach. Not her. Him. Not that it matters, but none of Dixie's people are men. Not one. Is the regular crew sick?

A few minutes later, we're southbound. An hour into our flight, Taylor freaks everyone out by crawling out from under my sweater and screaming like a cat in heat. After glancing around the cabin, she hides again. The pilot stares. Guess the crew's never seen a Daoine-Sìth kid before.

Courtenay holds both of our children while we wait for the second helicopter ride to begin.

By mid-afternoon, we land behind the Stepanova mansion. On the helipad. As always.

No breeze disturbs the snow. No footprints cross it. No distant traffic noise. Nothing. Complete silence except for the crew chatting. In English. Something ain't right.

Jazmine doesn't show. Nor anyone else. So I hand Taylor and Remie to my bondmate. "I'll see if I can find someone."

"Be careful," she says. Tension and concern flow across the bond. Yeah, I feel it too. The static in the air. Almost like a human version of dealan. Something's wrong. My hand wanders up to my throat, but my heart's back at Dixie's place.

I walk around the fountain and the pool area to the back doors. Before stepping inside, I study the helicopter in the distance, wondering what I'm missing. So what if the pilots are English-speaking men. Aren't most? And maybe everyone's busy inside. But something ain't right.

My asthma hasn't bothered me in months, but the air feels like a humid summer day. I take a deep breath and push against the glass doors. They're not locked, so I slip inside.

Stepan glances up from his seat at the table in the corner. A US marshal sits beside him. Stepan shakes his head at me. Get out, his eyes say. Run! Only it's not Stepan. Just some zombie replacement.

Courtenay stands beside the man, wearing a formal gown. Her beauty stuns. Except that she's been crying. Because of me. Yeah. Me. The bond trembles and stretches thin. Panic overwhelms me. I rush back outside.

There's no helicopter. Nothing at all in the summer sky. No time for it to have spun up its rotor blades. Just gone. My heart stutters. The bond stretches impossibly tight.

Flowers blossom in the urns beside the pool. The grass, though cut short is a dark green. The sun beats hot against my skin. I scream for it all to stop, for my love to return. But the bond snaps, and the recoil throws me across the yard. Blood flows from my nose and mouth. Unable to get enough oxygen, I crawl back toward the house, gasping for air.

Wild fragments of the bond swirl in the gathering darkness. I blink, but the light continues to fade. A soft goodbye whispers of Courtenay's death. And mine, soon enough.

I push myself to my feet and gather my skirts—satin and tulle with velvet trim and a crinoline petticoat—all soft pastel colors. I stumble away from the house, but my leg shrieks in pain. I fall. The urn tips—flowers, dirt, and all—into the pool and drags me with it.

Something holds me under the water. I struggle to escape, but without success. Does it matter? Courtenay's gone. The bond's shattered. So am I. Broken beyond repair. Sight fails. The silence whispers that it's too late. My heart thumps on in my temples, wanders through several erratic chords, and then stops.

Chapter Twenty

Out in the barren meadow, a few orphan sunbeams race across the withered grass, searching for the last remnants of fall. Wet snowflakes drift down from the sky, hoping to cover the frozen ground. Winter's coming. Soon.

My fingers press hard against the window pane so the frost creeps up my arms, down my chest, and into my soul. I lean my head against the glass till my breathing fogs the winterland vision. Cold seeps in but doesn't quite displace the emptiness.

Mamochka's hand enfolds mine in its hot embrace. "Come and see," she says. My mother urges me into the living room. To the great evergreen with its red star. Hand-painted ceramic ornaments decorate the limbs—Grandfather Frost, Snowmaiden, St Nicholas, Nutcracker. And—of course—the Nativity.

I rescue a wayward length of tinsel from the floor and hang it on the lowest branch. Nothing but pine needles and an old blanket lie under the tree. No presents there. Not this year. Yet Mamochka reaches high into the branches for a little box and smiles as she hands it to me. "Schastlivogo Rozhdestva, Annushka."

With shaking hands I hold my present. Then I snap open the lid of the small box to find a silver heart on a chain—the heirloom so precious to my mother. She's giving it to me! I stand there with my mouth wide, till Mamochka lifts the necklace from my open palm and hooks it around my neck. The heart glows warm against my chest. Then my mother kisses my forehead and smiles at me. Yes. Merry Christmas.

"Anya?" A woman in green scrubs draws me back to the present and away from the window. Jane blankets my cold fingers between her warm hands.

"Schastlivogo Rozhdestva," I say, though Mamochka's Christmas doesn't come till January.

The room's cold—at least close to the windows—but the air feels thick and warm around me now. My asthma's back. Maybe it's being around humans that makes it so difficult to get enough oxygen. Exhaustion drives my eyelids closed. My mind wanders across the barren wasteland toward the home I lost. Why struggle so hard, my soul? Relax—your body's dying.

I can feel the life seeping out of me. Darkness congeals in my lungs. My nurse smiles and hugs me. "You have guests," she says. She leads me to one of the little visiting rooms.

"Mamochka!" I squeal and rush to embrace Mrs. Andrews. Just holding someone—without Jazmine's drugs in my system—flows like soft music through my spirit. I can feel again. "Please tell me I get to go home with you."

But it's not Brit's mother. It's the blonde woman from the hospital room. The one who sat beside my bed for all those months as the doctors repaired me. And then through weeks of physical therapy. And counseling for emotional trauma. Yeah. That.

The woman gives me an enthusiastic bear hug before nodding. "It's true," she says. "I'm taking you home today. A long drive, though." She hands me one of my fifties farm-girl dresses. Repaired seams and all. I stare at it, till the woman asks me to go get dressed.

The nurse wheels me back to my room and waits while I change clothes. When she takes me out to the car, the blonde woman pops the trunk, but I don't have a suitcase or anything. Not so much as the heart Mamochka gave me. My spirit's missing even that small joy.

My love is dead—I know that for a certainty. Only microscopic particles of our bond remain—a fine dust gathering at the bottom of my empty soul. "We bond for life," Courtenay once said. "Daoine-Sìth survive not long the death of their bondmate." Yet I sit here, in a wheelchair, my crushed heart still beating.

The blonde woman opens the car door, and the nurse helps me into the front passenger seat.

What of Remie and Taylor? Alone in the world now, I suppose. How will I ever get back to them? The girls plead with me to come home, their voices high-pitched squeals. They tug on the hem of my kilt. I open my eyes again, but don't have enough energy to get out of the car. Nobody's gonna let me go back to Dixie's place, anyhow. Sorry, my babies. At least, we'll all be together in Heaven soon.

The blonde woman leans across the seat and kisses my cheek. "I'm so glad to have you back, Annushka. We worried that you might not survive."

I study the woman's features for a few quiet heartbeats, but remember nothing. Not her face. Not even her name. I don't know her. "Courtenay's dead," I say. That's all my soul cares about.

Frustration replaces the concern in the woman's eyes. "I'm sorry, honey, but she's been gone almost a year now. You need to move on."

No. Not that long. Yesterday. "I'm sick because they took her. They killed my bondmate. How am I supposed to recover from that?"

The woman shakes her head like I'm being a stubborn child. "No, Anya. The drugs your captors gave you resulted in severe memory loss. The doctors were able to restore function. Your brain's putting things back together now. But not necessarily the way events happened."

"We flew back to the Davydov estate on a helicopter." Yesterday.

"No, honey. After the police got you back from the traffickers, you fell into the pool at the Koshkin home. You nearly drowned."

My eyelids drift shut. Whatever happened, it left me with a slow leak in my soul and no way to repair it. Counselors—how much help can they be when they don't believe you? Okay, so, at this point, I'm not sure if any of my memories are real. But my spirit longs for Courtenay.

Hours pass as we roll along the interstate southbound. I breathe through an open mouth, because it seems easier. After the darkness fades, my eyes wander back toward the blonde woman. "I'm sorry, ma'am. I don't remember anything. Would you help me? Please?"

She eyes me—at first like I'm being obnoxious again—but eventually nods. "Your name's Anna Ilyinichna Koshkina—Ilya and Iseabail's only child. Courtenay Koshkina was your cousin. The two of you were close, but apparently something terrible happened. She killed herself, and you tried to follow."

Ilya—the blond-haired dude I met so long ago? "My father's a US marshal?"

She doesn't glance my way this time, but nods. "Yes."

"I'm adopted?"

The woman eyes me again. Like why would I ask such a stupid question? "No," she says. "But since your mother died, you've spent more time with me—and my daughter Brit—than with your father."

"Brit." No. Just no. But I close my eyes and wait for whatever comes next.

Silence, mostly. An hour later, we turn into the driveway of a house I recognize well—on 14th Avenue in New Brighton. The old red brick two-story that the Andrews owned. Still do, I guess. At least in whatever alternate universe I'm stuck in now.

Brit—and this copy does resemble my bestie—the girl looks up from pulling weeds in the garden. When the blonde woman opens the passenger door, I slide my legs out and wobble to my feet. The neighborhood cat—the one that was supervising Brit—runs over to me and rubs against my legs.

Brit saunters my way, pulls me close, and kisses my cheek. "Welcome, home, Annushka," she says. Then she takes my hand—the way the real Brit used to. Yeah. Exactly like that. The girl nods at her mother, "I'll take her upstairs, Ma." So I follow my bestie inside and up the stairway.

Everything's the same. Everything. Except the people. After Brit finishes the tour, I walk back to the work room and settle in to the old wicker couch. A brief search for my unfinished watercolors finds nothing but my paints and paper. On a hunch, I walk down the hallway to Brit's room and look under the bed. When I slide the storage box out and remove the top, I find my watercolor landscape there. Well, I guess it's mine. The thing has more details than before. Or

maybe it's because I know the place so well now that it seems different.

After I return the watercolor, I search for a nightgown. There's
one in the dresser drawer. The same dresser drawer. Yeah. The
vintage négligée—nylon and chiffon and comfy soft—with the same
small tears that mean you can't sell it. It's not suppertime yet, but I
change clothes anyhow.

So they just replaced the people. What happened to the real Brit
and her mom? Do they exist on this timeline? Or has something
happened to my brain as well as my memories?

I walk down the hallway to my closet, but it's full of supplies, so
I wander back to Brit's room and hang my fifties dress in her closet.
My embroidered peasant top is there. So is the fancy dress they gave
me. Repairs and all. No mud stains. I missed the prom, though. And
my springtime.

I crawl into bed. It squeaks as I roll over, and again when I
reach up to turn off the lamp. Courtenay's dead. The Andrews have
been replaced by zombies. Months are gone from my memory—and
my life. But this bed's the same. Am I insane to let that comfort me?
The mattress and pillow are old friends. I don't have much else. So I
close my eyes and dream of Courtenay and our children.

Chapter Twenty-One

In the silent darkness I cling to my bondmate, like some hopeless toddler who lost her mommy. Grief overwhelms my dreams, keeps me from deep slumber. My soul aches for my love. And my children.

Taylor and Remie! I call their names in the night. My bondmate quiets me with a kiss. "They're fine," she says. Though my body longs for Courtenay's touch, no life flows from her embrace. No cinnamon fragrance. No blue sparks fall from her fingertips. No bond between us. My love's dead. Gone. I lie back down and close eyes that have already shed a lifetime of tears.

Awareness creeps back as the early morning light ripples across the ceiling. The crisp morning air stirs the drapes. I breathe deep of the cool goodness. Brit—if she slept in the room with me—rose early. I roll out of bed and stretch my legs. For the moment, at least, I feel human. No. Healthy. 'Cause I'm not sure about the human part.

I dress in my peasant top and bellbottom jeans, brush out my hair, and walk down the stairway. No one appears to be home, so I find cereal in the cupboard and milk in the fridge. Bacon and eggs would be nice, but I can't waste energy on such things.

The doorbell rings as I'm rinsing my bowl. I find a place for it in the dishwasher and walk down the hallway to the back porch. A note on the door says,

> Anya,
>
> I asked Dylan to spend some time with you. He is, after all, your boyfriend. I explained that you've forgotten much, and the parts you do remember aren't assembled properly. He promised to help.
>
> —Clara

I pull the door open to find a boy holding a motorcycle helmet. Not Dylan, though. This guy's much too cute to impersonate him. Whoever controls the space-time continuum obviously couldn't find a suitable replacement.

The boy leans close and kisses my cheek. "Welcome home, Annushka," he says. "Your aunt asked me to spend the day with you. She said you'd forgotten some things."

This boy loves me. His eyes overflow with tenderness. Along with pain and a touch of fear. A straight boy—transparent about his feelings. Sorry, kid, but I'm gonna hurt you eventually. 'Cause I'm not into boys. Not even really cute ones who love me. I glance back down the hallway toward the kitchen, remembering my Dylan's invitation to the prom. Yeah. Okay. So maybe I should be nice to this one. For the sake of mine.

I sigh, take the hand he offers, and follow him to his motorcycle. Whatever drugs Jazmine gave me—whatever the doctor implanted in my abdomen—whatever destroyed my bond with Courtenay—it all left me with a deep emptiness and a serious need for human companionship. Not sex—mind you—just physical closeness. A gentle touch. And perhaps conversation. So I climb on the motorcycle in back of Dylan and pull myself tight against him. That's what I need most right now.

We ride north on Route 65 and east on 588. Yeah. I could drive to Brush Creek Park with my eyes closed. The road hasn't changed at all. Just the season.

When we get there, we drive past the soccer fields and over the bridges. They're still repairing the second one. Same orange barrels as a year ago. We continue beyond the picnic areas and the tennis courts. Past the same old playground. Around the chain that's supposed to keep vehicles out. Across the old covered bridge, and along the far bank. To the same spot my Dylan took me a year ago.

I walk down to the creek's edge, sit on the granite boulder, and watch for the chipmunks I saw the last time. But this isn't like it was then. I was six inches taller, had just gotten my heart necklace back from my sister, and was playing on Dylan's team as Anatoli—a boy. One of his best players. Now I get tired just waking up in the morning.

Dylan sits beside me and slinks an arm around my waist. "Where do we begin?" he says.

Does it matter? I'm stuck here with a trashed memory and a dying body. I lean my head against his shoulder. "Courtenay," I say, without thinking. Like I expect the boy to understand that it's her I miss. And not him.

Dylan kisses me on the cheek and then sighs. "I'm sorry," he says. "I know you loved her." He picks up a stone and throws it into the water. "Your aunt and uncle adopted her maybe two years ago."

"When did she die?"

He stares at me for a moment, tenderness filling his eyes. "A year ago. They say she took something—I'm not sure what—something that caused her body to shut down. Slowly."

I shake my head. "Courtenay wouldn't have taken drugs or poison. No matter what. She wasn't like that."

The boy reaches over and squeezes my hand. A gentle caress, actually. Like he really is my boyfriend or something. Then he sighs. "Her family took her down to Cozumel, hoping the sunshine and salt air would help. They say she seemed happy enough, but she walked out past the breakers and was never seen again."

Yeah. I get it. "She gave herself to the sea." I understand why a Daoine-Sìth would do that. I'd do the same thing right now. I stand and walk along the bank. Not far—I haven't the energy. But I need to clear out the cobwebs. So I stare down into the rushing water and imagine it flowing around me. Taking me away from here. To Paradise.

Dylan slides an arm around my waist again. This time he hugs me and draws my head down against his shoulder. For a few minutes, at least, the darkness fades.

Then a fat raindrop hits me and spatters. A second and third follow. We'll be soaked if we don't take cover somewhere. The boy urges me toward his motorcycle. "Let's grab something to eat," he says. So we drive out of the park, searching for clear skies. Twenty minutes later, we pull to a stop in front of Melody's Diner. Yeah. The same one.

"Anya!" The waitress rushes across the room and hugs me like we're good friends. Like I didn't end up being drugged and raped because of her aunt. Unless my memory is that far off. Which it could be. A sigh works its way up out of my gut. Does it matter? Courtenay's dead. I'm dying, and there's no ocean in Beaver County.

I follow Dylan to the corner booth and sit across from the boy. Yeah. This is the one where my Dylan asked me to the prom. It has the same graffiti carved into the table top. The same initials in a heart. Hope they're still in love.

When Melody comes to our booth, we order the usual. I'm hoping the burgers are as yummy as I remember. After the waitress leaves, Dylan leans toward me. "Courtenay died a year ago, but you never seemed to accept that. Six weeks ago, you disappeared. People thought you'd run away, but when the police brought you back, they said you'd been trafficked."

Darkness gathers around me. And fear. Of being alone and crazy. Of Courtenay really being gone. Muscles tighten the way they did when I knew my father was going to beat me. I raise both hands in front of me and shake my head. "I was gone for almost a year."

The boy's eyebrows climb up his forehead. "Two weeks, Annushka. And then in the hospital and PT for a month after you fell into the pool."

When I shake my head again, he pulls out his phone and sets it in front of me.

All I need to see is the date. I'm a year ahead of his reality. Terror seizes me. My breathing stops. What are the odds that they control the Internet as well as my memory? The boy stares—pain and tender concern etched across his face. I push the phone back across the table in surrender. I'm not missing a spring and summer. I lived through nine months that haven't happened yet.

Dylan reaches across the table and caresses my hand. "It's okay, Annuska. You don't have to remember anything the way it happened. Just accept that you're here. With friends."

Yeah. Friends. Great. Okay, so he is kinda cute. "You play soccer?"

The boy's smile returns. "Yeah. Our team has a match tomorrow. Pretty sure Brit will be there. Why don't you come?"

"You're the captain?" My Dylan would have said so right out.

"Yeah." Like it's nothing special. He reaches for his phone again. "Hey. I have some photos you might like to see." He fiddles around for a moment and then hands it to me again.

On the screen is a selfie of him. With me. He's wearing a navy blue suit. A nice one, but not a tux. The boy's cute. I get that. Me? I've got on the dress Brit's mom gave me. Someone did a decent job on my makeup. Brit, probably. And I'm smiling. Yeah. Like being with Dylan at a party is the best thing ever.

What happened to that me? Is she happy now? Or dying slowly? "Thanks," I say—like I mean it—and hand the boy his phone.

Black clouds roll across the sky outside. Lightning flashes in the distance. A nice boy—one who loves me—sits across the table from me, and all I can think about is Courtenay. "Where was she from?" I say. Like he'll know who I'm talking about without saying her name.

The boy's face saddens. His eyes say it's because he cares about me. And I'm clearly grieving for the girl. He draws in a deep breath and sighs. "She said she was born on an island. Somewhere in Scotland." His lips twitch up into a smile. "You joked once that she was a banshee."

"Bean-sìthe," I say. "Fairy maiden. Yeah. Her cèile—her bondmate—must have died." I refuse to cry again. To have the life flow out of my soul. So I watch the storm drift past. And slow my breathing. She's gone. Forever.

Dylan caresses my hand. "She's gone. But you're still here."

"I shouldn't be." But I nod. For him. And wait for the sky to clear.

After a while, Melody approaches. She stands in silence next to me. In the window, her eyes show compassion. And pain. I turn to face her. "You have family in Erie, don't you?" An aunt who sells young women into slavery.

Sadness overwhelms the girl's face, and she shakes her head. "No. Not any more. My aunt died last month."

"Sorry. I didn't know."

She turns to me and offers a sad smile. "That's okay."

The sun peeks through the overcast. A last few raindrops fall. My eyes wander from the window to Dylan. He nods, picks up the helmets, and leads me back outside to his motorcycle. After he wipes the seat dry, I slide on behind him and snuggle up close.

When the boy stops in the driveway at the Andrews home, I get off the bike and hand his helmet back to him. "Thanks," I say. What else should I do? He's supposed to be my boyfriend. The guy actually seems to love me. I lean close, but have to wait for him to pull off his helmet before I can kiss his cheek.

A smile spreads across the boy's face. "Hope to see you at the game," he says. His eyes insist on his love, but he does nothing more. Just a sigh before he puts on his helmet again and drives off.

"He is kinda cute." My bestie pushes the screen door open.

"Yeah. For a boy." I give her a quick hug before going upstairs to the work room. I clear off the top of the sewing machine cabinet and get out a pad of watercolor paper. The cheap stuff is all I can afford.

I begin a new sketch. Of Brit. For her birthday. This time, I'll be more careful. Well, the pencil and paper stage isn't my problem. It's trying to do the watercolor part of a portrait. I go for too much detail and end up spoiling the painting.

Half an hour later, Brit walks into the room. I hold up the sketch. Her smile warms my soul. Some day I'll actually give her a completed watercolor.

Rather than open up my paints, I do a second sketch—another attempt at an oriental landscape. This one with a group of herons as the main focus.

Time passes weird when I'm painting. What seems like five minutes, and I look up to find Brit standing there, pointing at her watch. Time to go.

I blink at her. "I thought the match was tomorrow."

The girl just shakes her head. This is tomorrow. So I slide both drawings back inside the pad and put everything away.

Most of the time, Brush Creek Park is only twenty minutes away from New Brighton. Today, though, there's a wreck. So we wait while the police do their thing. And an ambulance comes. Eventually, a police officer tells us to turn around. So we backtrack to Concord Circle Road and take Glendale to the park.

The soccer field doesn't have bleachers. Do they ever? So I get a lawn chair out of Brit's trunk and set it up beside the field. The teams are already there, so I wave at Dylan.

He shouts to someone in the crowd and comes running over to where I'm sitting. I stand up for him and kiss him on the cheek. For my Dylan. And because the guy's being super nice to me even though I don't remember him.

His smile becomes a grin when a tall redhead appears out of the crowd. A tall, impossibly thin girl. With green eyes. I stare way longer than is polite.

"Annushka, this is Courtenay's sister, Anastasie."

The girl nods and places her chair beside mine. I continue to stare. She could be my clone. Back when I was a tall redhead. If I ever was. Or maybe I just dreamed that I was Courtenay's sister. A sigh works up out of my gut. Does it matter? My bondmate's dead.

Dylan continues to talk. "She's in foster care in Beaver Falls. Plays for the Tigers—the girls' basketball team." The boy kisses me on the cheek and wanders back out to the rest of his team.

"Anya?" The girl reaches over and presses something hot into my open hand. "My sister asked me to make certain that you got this."

A heart, no doubt. My gaze flicks down to my hand. 'Cause I need to know for sure. Yeah—glowing silver, with a pastel blue St.

Andrew's cross embedded deep within the metal. Gaelic writing on the back. Yeah. Identical. Its warmth flows into my heart.

When I look up again, Anastasie's gone. Not into the crowd. 'Cause there ain't one. No game. No players. Nothing. Just Dylan in one direction—sitting on his motorcycle—and Brit in the other—leaning against her car. Waiting to give me a ride home.

A single tear scurries down my face. I put on the necklace, nod goodbye to Dylan, and then pick up my chair and walk toward Brit.

All the way back to the Andrews place, I roll the heart between my fingers. Some small part of me is whole again—something within me healed. Mamochka used to say that her necklace had been passed down—mother to daughter—for at least six generations. I gave it to Pasha once. 'Cause getting her away from Papa would save her life. I let Giselle take it from me once. But it's mine forever now.

As soon as Brit parks the car, I open the door and wobble across the driveway to the back porch. Okay, so I'm not completely healed. My bestie rushes to catch up. "You okay?" she says.

I give her a long hug. "Sorry," I whisper to the girl. "I'm tired. Think I'll take a nap before supper." Dark clouds hit me as I walk up the stairway to our bedroom. My free hand wanders up to the heart at my throat and holds it tight. For a moment, at least, I feel better again.

The peasant blouse I hang in the closet. I fold my jeans and find room for them in the dresser. My bra follows. Then I get out one of the old nightgowns, slide it on, and crawl into bed. A gray haze flows over me. I close my eyes and surrender to darkness.

I run down the cobblestone pathway, chasing Courtenay. Okay, so the drugs increase my need for physical contact. I get that. But I'd love the girl anyhow without them. My body surges with joy and adrenaline. I breathe deep of the crisp air and let go of everything that slows me down.

Courtenay leads me through the orchard—the one from my early paintings—the one I spent hours of my childhood wandering through—searching in vain for my mother. Courtenay dodges behind a tree, pauses for a moment, laughs at me, and moves on. When she finally stops, we both stand in front of my mother's statue. Panting.

The girl smiles at me again, taunting. Yeah. She's faster. And more agile. Even though I was better at soccer than most of the boys on my team. "I'll be the male," Courtenay says, as though physical abilities determine that. There are plenty of strong women and weak men.

No. She'd never say it, but she's purebred Daoine-Sìth and I'm half human. That slows me down a bit. I bend over, rest my hands on my knees, and cough out mucous. Not asthma—that seems to have gone away. But I still have some pollen allergies.

I smile back at her. "Who knows? After we bond, I might be the one who becomes male."

Father—the one who carries the seven or eight babies that come from that first bonding kiss. Mother—she breast feeds the kids. Someday I'll understand Daoine-Sìth biology. Someday I might even believe that I'm not living in a drug-induced fantasy.

My leg twitches and then cramps. I sit up. In bed. At Brit's. Alone.

Courtenay's gone. Or never existed. My body quivers with the need to move—something I haven't felt since—since before we bonded. And my body changed back to petite and feminine with large breasts.

Boobs! My heart races in a sudden panic. I let the sheet slide down. Yeah. Mine are small again. Like when I had red hair. And could run faster than the boys. I breathe in ragged spasms through an open mouth. Fear and adrenaline—not asthma.

I'm at Brit's tonight. Tomorrow morning, a US marshal will try to convince me to go home with him. In the afternoon, Dylan and I ride out to Brush Creek Park and then have lunch at Melody's Diner. Monday, I go to a doctor. Have my blood drawn. Seventeen dead. Tuesday, I ride up to Erie with Melody.

I slide out of bed and pull off my nightgown. In the mirror, a tall, skinny redhead frowns at me. My eyes do a slow blink. My whole body shakes. I plead with Mrs. Andrews' God to help me understand what's happening to me.

"Anya?" Brit's voice echoes down the hallway. My muscles quiver. I grab one of my old fifties dresses from the closet and hold it up against me. Not like that will hide my red hair. Or my emerald eyes. Or my being six inches taller than I was this morning. The girl's seen me naked often enough, but like a guilty little kid, I need to hide.

My bestie pokes her head into the room. "You feeling better now?" Her eyes scan me. She smiles as if nothing's different. Nothing at all. A glance at the mirror proves her right. My body's the one I had this morning. Petite. Feminine. Pale blonde hair. Blue eyes. Pretty. But totally insane.

"Yeah. Guess so," I say, though my arms shake. Was I dreaming? My body remembers wanting to run. Muscles twitch like rubber bands wound tight. My asthma—at least for now—seems far away.

"Will you help me with dinner?" the girl says. "Ma's on the phone with your father. They may be a while."

"Yeah. Sure." I lay the dress on the bed and find a bra and clean panties in the dresser. When I turn around again, my bestie's still standing there, watching me.

"Sorry," the girl says. "It's just that—you—" Brit shakes her head. "For a moment I thought you were someone else." She turns and walks away.

Chapter Twenty-Two

Shoes click across the hardwood floor downstairs. The back door squeaks open and closed again. Brit moans, rolls over, and sits up. I slide out of bed and push back the curtain. Yeah. A black Escalade sits out front. No squad car, though.

Brit presses close beside me. "That's your father's car, ain't it?"

"Yeah. Guess so. He's a US marshal?"

She nods, but her eyes wonder if I'll ever be normal again. I pull her close long enough to kiss her cheek. For my old Brit—wherever she is. And the version of me that this Brit used to know. 'Cause I'm hoping we can all get back home someday. Or at least find sanity again.

After I get dressed, I wander down the stairway to greet my father. Not sure who I was expecting, but my heart freezes when I step into the kitchen. "He found you," the voices whisper. "He'll hurt you again."

No. This man's not my biological father. Not anything like Kyrill Gilyov, if I can believe the love and concern in the man's eyes.

He stands and crosses the room in three quick steps. My entire body goes rigid, but the man scoops me up off the floor and into a wild bear hug. After a moment, my muscles begin to relax. Kyrill would already have found an excuse to hit me.

The man releases his grip, but rests a hand on my shoulder. "I'm sorry that I can't take you home yet, but I wanted to see how you were doing. You look awesome. A little tired, perhaps. How are you feeling?"

Kyrill never treated me with kindness. Not even in front of other people. My mouth works—I want to answer, but words fail me. So I return his smile and kiss the man on the cheek. Like I would a father who loves me. Even though the dude looks way too much like Kyrill.

He motions me toward the kitchen table, then pulls out a chair. So I sit. And eat breakfast. Bacon, eggs, and toast—the usual fare for the Andrews. Same as in my previous life. And today, I'm starving. Like I spent the night playing soccer. Or chasing Courtenay.

The man seems content to watch me. So I pause between bites and smile at him.

"Clara says you don't remember anything. Or at least that your memory is flawed. Do you mind if I share a little history with you?"

The kindness in his eyes and voice sweep me away. Kyrill. What a difference this guy would have made. My chest tightens. Not asthma. Just awe at having a decent father. I still can't say anything, though, so I nod again.

The man leans toward me. "Your mother and I were divorced while she was still pregnant with you. To be honest, I didn't realize she was with child. My own fault, that." He nods, like he's agreeing with someone's objection. My Kyrill would never have admitted he was wrong. The guy smiles at me again. "Iseabail moved to Canada to work at a secret research facility. Genetics, I think. We didn't talk about it much."

He straightens in the chair and nods again. "About two years ago, she was killed—I still don't know the circumstances of her death. But I fought long and hard to get custody of my daughter." His eyes wander toward the ceiling. He pauses for a moment before continuing.

"Apparently, you and your mother were living in a secluded part of the institution. Anyway, when I brought you back to Beachwood, Ohio, you had so much trouble in school that I agreed to let Clara homeschool you for a while. And I talked to your uncle about adopt-ing a playmate."

His eyes return to mine. Sadness overwhelms everything else. "Courtenay was born in Scotland and seemed to share your interest in folklore. Daoine-Sìth, you called them. She claimed that she had been born on an island of elves."

The man takes a long sip from his coffee. "The two of you grew close rather quickly. Then something happened. Her physical health deteriorated as did your emotional state. Courtenay died. You ran away. Or so we thought."

The man reaches across the table to rest his hand on mine. "Whatever happened, the police found you in New York State at a place that buys and sells young women. You'd been drugged and raped. They filmed pornography with you. Who knows what else they did?" His eyes wander again. He shakes his head. "I'm sorry. I should have been there for you."

I move closer. He stands and draws me into an awesome bear hug. A father who truly loves me. I hold him tight. Till he eases away and says that he needs to leave.

Chapter Twenty-Three

My health continues to decline as the weeks pass. I'm not well enough to be at school, okay? But staying at home sucks almost as much. Especially with Brit in classes, her mother at work, and me alone with nothing to do. I'd help with household chores, but I don't have the stamina. So I put up with what I must.

A bell marks the end of French class. Lucy grins at me and whispers, "Pédé," as she walks past. French slang for faggot. Someone else snickers, but I don't bother looking up. I wait for the rest of my classmates to leave before closing my notebook.

I trudge down the hallway to the library and drop my books on a table close to the windows. Not enough energy for anything more. Not enough oxygen. Not enough whatever else.

Ms. Hollinger eases the door closed. "May I see you for a moment?"

I push myself up out of my seat, wait for the gray haze to pass, and then shuffle over to her desk. School policy's supposed to be LGBT friendly. Supposed to accommodate preferred names and pronouns. But apparently the school board—or some fake family organization—thinks I should be an exception. I'm not allowed in the locker room with the girls. So I have an extra Study Hall.

The librarian eyes me like I'm some juvenile delinquent. Yeah—well—I might could be that. The woman rests her elbows on the desk and leans toward me. "This school has a zero-tolerance policy on bullying. If you have any trouble, I want to know."

"Yeah. Sure." But if I complain, things will get worse. I shuffle back to my desk—out of breath now—and collapse into my chair.

After my vision clears, I pick up my History text. Might as well at least look like I care about school. When I open the book, a white flower falls to my desk. Jasmine, I think. There's also a small card that says Happy Birthday. Yeah. Sweet. They're almost a month off. Not that it matters.

My heart bleeds again—great red drops of loneliness—and the darkness within me grows. Too many drugs. Too much bouncing. No energy for pointless games. I'm not gonna make it till I'm eighteen and free of this prison.

My eyes scan the walls, desperate for some reason to live. To take one more breath. A poster shows the school's football schedule. Like I care. September 1st, the calendar says.

Le premier septembre. Dixie's birthday. Today. If the woman exists. My eyes lose focus as I stare at the wall. The second hand sweeps past twelve again. I pick up the flower and examine it. A year ago—to the day—Melody and Grace sold me to Stepan. Jazmine took me to...

No. Not a year ago. Today. Jazmine's gotta be here. Now. But where? The girl should know I didn't testify against the Stepanovas. Or snitch on Dixie. I wander up to Ms. Hollinger's desk and stand there, squirming. "I need to use the restroom. Stat."

She eyes me like I'm an idiot—which I probably am—but the woman jerks her head toward the door. I grab the flower and slide out into the hallway. I can't run. If I walk too fast, I'll pass out. But I push myself. Till my lungs burn. Till my vision fades to gray again. Till I'm just inside the front entrance. And facing Dylan.

He shakes his head and motions for me to sit on the bench in the hallway. "Anastasie's gone," the boy says. Like I made her disappear. "She gave you the heart, didn't she?"

I slump down on the seat, exhausted. "She," I say—in a whisper. "Me, actually, I think. In another dimension. Or something." I pull the necklace out from under my top. The heart's glowing again. "Did she say where she got it?"

Dylan slides in beside me, his frown gone. "No. Sorry. She just said that you were the rightful owner." He glances toward the door. "You're leaving? If you go, I'll never see you again."

His eyes hold such pain that I almost lie to the boy. Almost. "Yeah. I think I can get back to wherever it is I came here from." I take several deep breaths, hoping to clear the fog. It doesn't work. So, yeah. Honesty. "I'm dying," I say. "For the same reason Courtenay did, I think."

"Can't the doctors do anything?"

"No. Nothing they tried while I was in rehab helped. And, twice, the drugs they gave me resulted in severe allergic reactions." My shoulders rise in a careless shrug. "My body's different."

The boy pulls me close and kisses my forehead. "I don't want to lose you, Annushka."

Love. Yeah. Without drugs. Only it's another Anya the boy wants. So I shake my head. "I'm sorry, Dylan. I don't belong here. Maybe your Anya will come back if I leave." I push myself to my feet, stagger over to the door and push. My weight's enough to open it and get me outside.

Snow. Well that sucks. In September? A chill runs through me— not unlike the first wave of withdrawal. If that's coming, I'll be dead before I reach the parking lot. And I really should kiss this Dylan goodbye. Or something. Anything to take away his pain. And some of mine.

I stumble back inside. The boy's not there. Neither's the bench. When some part of my brain recognizes the place as my old school in Beaver Falls, my eyelids close in pain. Only my hand on the wall keeps me from falling. I haven't cried in months, but a blob of water drips down my face and splashes on the floor.

Outside again, I scan the parking lot, seeking an old Chevy, one nobody would bother stealing. Like the rusty sedan that just stopped in the drop-off area. Yeah. Exactly like that car.

My gaze drifts across the school grounds, and then wanders out to Jazmine's Chevy again. Hold me against my will. Drug me. Rape me. Film pornography with me. Tattoo my face. Sell me to a pedophile. Give me psycho drugs that make me hallucinate. I'd be a moron to do anything but call out the National Guard. My hand digs down into my purse, but—oh, yeah—no cell phone allowed. Well that sucks.

At least being a Stepanova was never boring. A desperate long-ing billows up out of my soul—with Courtenay I was happy. But my bondmate's dead. Or she existed only in a drug-induced fantasy. I step down off the curb and creep toward the old Chevy. Jazmine's not gonna make the ruins of my life any worse.

"I missed you, Stepanova." Jazmine steps out of her car and hugs me. The real Jazmine. Not some zombie replica. Then the girl kisses me on the cheek. Like we're sisters or something. Instead of —well, yeah—that.

She brushes a fingertip across my cheek. Where my tattoo used to be. "What should I call you now?" she says.

Jazmine never asked me that before. Like I ever had a choice. I glance back toward the school again. Mamochka's gone. I'll never see Brit or her mom again. With my health issues, I'm still not gonna survive very long. What do I want?

Kyrill strolls out of the main doors of the school building. Or at least his ghost. Yeah, death waits for me back there, only a few foot-steps behind me now. The zombies know my name.

What should Jazmine call me? I grin like an angry shark and state my name for the record—just like I'm in court—"Madame Anas-tasie Bijou Dubois."

A mischievous grin creeps across the girl's face. "Zinaida just lost a wager. I have some things to tell you. Mind if we go some-where and talk?"

Again with the questions. Am I really free to say no? To go back? Fear blossoms at the possibility that I could walk away right now and never see her again. I don't want to die alone. That much of the need for human contact still burns deep within. Not from her stupid drugs either.

While I delay, the girl's smile fades to disappointment. "I'll bring you back here. Or drop you off at your house."

"No. I'm good." I pull her into a quick hug. "I'm just not used to you giving me any choices."

Her wicked smile returns for a moment. "You outrank me now, Madame Dubois."

As we pull out onto the highway, I glance back one last time and don't quite resist the urge to raise a middle finger in the school's general direction. I so hope I never return there. Or see any of them again. Ever.

Jazmine pulls off at the local airport exit and parks in front of a quiet little restaurant. After we order, she retrieves an envelope from her purse and slides it across the table. "Zinaida bet that you wouldn't want these."

I worry open the envelope and dump out its contents. The first item's a Canadian passport for Anastasie Bijou Dubois with a nice photo of my face and all the correct information. Then there's two certified copies of a birth certificate for Anastasie Bijou Dubois.

Jazmine's looking like my mother now—all happy for her daughter. I stand up just far enough to lean across the table and kiss the girl on the lips. The drugs may be gone, but my body still remembers hers. And I hope hers does mine.

When I sit down again, her face turns more serious. "Unfortunately, if you show those to anyone here, they'll likely confiscate them. If you come back home, though, they should keep you from ever being sent here again."

"Dixie wants me?" Do I really need to be the old woman's plaything? Or even Jazmine's costar? How can those possibly be any kid's two best choices for a home?

"She's dying. Zinaida promised her I'd find you and ask you to come home long enough for Dixie to say goodbye."

Or have someone bury me with her so that she'll have a sex toy in the afterlife. A week up north without Courtenay or the children, and I may beg Dixie to take me with her.

Better than dying alone. I draw in a deep breath and let it out slowly. I am so gonna regret this. But… "Let's go."

Jazmine hugs me again. Tight. Like we'll never see each other again. A short drive takes us to a commercial building at the general aviation airport. Jazmine leads me inside and says a few words to the woman behind the counter. Then she turns to me again. "One more thing," she says. The girl smiles like a shark smelling blood. "Your sister's waiting for me to take her back home.

"Pasha?" I'd almost forgotten that I had a twin.

"Yes. She's the one who told us where you were."

I stare at Jazmine, mouth open, till she says, "If you run, the Koshkins will eventually track you down. Unless, of course, they don't know you're gone."

Why did you do all of this, Pasha? You're back where you started. And I'm screwed.

After Jazmine leaves, I show the lady at the desk my passport. She takes me out into the hangar to a private jet. The all-female crew speaks French. Of course. And I still don't. But the women smile and nod when I sit in a plush leather seat and buckle in. One drapes a heavy cashmere blanket over me before walking to the front of the aircraft.

I flew without hope the first time. Because I knew my life was short. Now I don't remember why I thought that mattered. Losing my freedom and my future hurt less than Mamochka's death. Or Kyrill's unbending rejection of his daughter.

I have hope now. Not because I trust Jazmine. Or Dixie. I know who I am, though, and—however this works out—this time I choose it.

I know who I am. Well, okay, so I'm not sure that I'm even human. And may or may not have children. I close my eyes and relax. None of it matters right now.

Hours pass. By the time the turbines spin down, we're parked in front of a snow-covered but familiar hangar. One of the crew hands me a for-serious cashmere-lined suede parka. I slip it on and wait for the woman to open the door.

This time, I walk down the steps alone and into the depths of winter. Ice crystals scurry across the runway. Barren trees sway in the wind. I pull the softness of my parka tight and wait for the approaching helicopter to land.

My world goes crazy white and bone-chilling cold for a moment as the aircraft touches down, bounces softly, and settles in.

Before the blades stop, I duck my head and run toward the open door.

Warmth, a leather seat, and the whine of turbines welcome me. After we're airborne, I notice a Thermos in a holder by my seat. A little card says, "Chocolat Chaud." Hot cocoa?

Have you ever had a Frozen Russian?

They wouldn't. Would they? Do I care? I drink deep of the frothy goodness, lean back into the seat, and hope Mrs. Andrews—wherever she is—is still praying for me. Guess I trust her God more than I do anyone else.

A soft whistle joins the music as we fly north over small islands, pine trees, and unbroken sheets of ice. The sun's reflection shatters into a million sparkling red and gold fragments under a darkening sky. An hour—maybe two—pass in a winterland dream before we reach the crystal fields of Dixie's estate and begin our descent into a maelstrom of snow.

For a moment, a solitary clearing in the storm reveals a stone landing pad below us. Then nothing. Long-forgotten vertigo rocks me. I clutch at the armrests of my seat. But a single gentle bounce ends our flight.

The pilot opens the door a crack, but shakes her head when I pop my safety harness. "Attends ici," she says. So I lean back into my seat and wait. While the wind howls. And the air grows frigid. Till my breath hangs in a frozen cloud before me, and my lungs ache.

Eventually, a flashlight wobbles toward me. The door swings open, and the pilot urges me out into the swirling madness. "Vers la lumière!" the woman shouts. She grabs my arm and turns off her flashlight.

Vertigo hits again for an instant before the world stabilizes. I step down into the snow. And utter darkness. Toward the light. What light? I can't see anything. Not the woman beside me. Not my own hands. Nothing. But the pilot tugs me off to the right a little. Then left. I hold my other hand out in front of me and shuffle along. Till the darkness glows with the dimmest hope of light. An ancient oak door swings open then, and we stumble into overwhelming warmth and brightness.

Chapter Twenty-Four

Before my eyes recover, I'm buried in a sea of squealing children, every last one wanting to crawl over me. Two help me remove my parka. Another grabs my hand and guides me to a sofa in front of a fireplace.

Embers float up the chimney. The fire crackles. Exhaustion drops me deep into the plush but impossibly hot cushions. Warmth returns to my body.

Tiny feet patter across the floor and stop in front of me. My youngest stands there—not much larger than a Blythe doll—barely knee high. Her tiny arms hold up a toy ceramic cup filled with creamy goodness. "Soupe aux pois, Maman?"

So it wasn't all a fantasy. But am I ready to be Mamochka for my little girls? That would mean staying here. Forever. 'Cause no place else accepts kids that don't even look human. I take the offering from Remie's hands. "Merci beaucoup, ma belle."

Timid pink eyes stare at me through a wild disarray of white hair. A desperate fear burns there. I don't want to die alone, they whisper.

"Ça ira, ma puce," I say, then tip my head toward the empty space beside me. "Assieds-toi."

The girl scrambles up on the seat and snuggles hard against me, digging into my peasant top. Yeah. Leaving here alone's gonna be a problem. Not that I have any choice but to stay till the snow's gone. I lean back into the cushion and swallow the mouthful of soup. Somebody here knows how to cook. No, seriously. Who makes split-pea soup that actually tastes good?

A few minutes after I set aside the empty cup, Taylor approaches. "Mémère. Elle..." She glances back toward the far end of the room. At the floor. Anywhere but my face. When our eyes do meet, hers drip with a mournful emptiness that shreds my heart.

"Elle te demande, Maman," she says, her voice not much above a whisper.

I move Remie to my hip. With my free arm, I pull Taylor close, and we wander off toward Dixie's rooms. Yeah, I know the way there.

The pilot stands in front of her door—like an armed guard. "Au lit, mes petites." She shakes her head and waves the girls away.

Remie starts crying, but drops to the floor, and scampers away. Taylor glances at me before following her sister. "I'm sorry, my little ones." A sigh lifts my chest, but I can't help them. Even if I had a place for my children, I wouldn't survive long enough to take them there. Without much hope, I step into Dixie's bedroom suite.

A frail and ancient woman sits at her desk, writing something. The door clicks shut behind me. I stand in silence, waiting, mouth open, each breath more difficult than the last.

For all she's done to me—and to her own children—I should hate this woman. Perhaps I do. But God's vengeance isn't far off. Even so, anger and sorrow threaten to overwhelm me. I struggle to hold back the tears. And the Russian curses. Yeah, Kyrill taught me those.

Dixie pushes herself to her feet and faces me. "You're dying," she says—as though it matters not. "The children will follow not long after."

English. I almost miss that part. So natural. Not even an accent. Yes, I do hate her.

She stops an arm's length away. No embrace. No contact. But her eyes examine my soul. "My death is certain," the woman says. "Days—perhaps a few weeks." She motions me toward a chair, and then returns to her desk and sits down. "However unlikely, there remains hope for you."

Her eyes drift closed. Minutes pass with only a clock ticking. Till someone knocks. Dixie opens her eyes. "Please let her in."

I ease the door open. Giselle nods to the pilot, and then steps inside. She walks over to Dixie, strokes the old woman's hair, and then paces the room for a minute before facing me. "You're brave to come back here, girl."

"Why? What have I to lose?"

She starts to say something, but then bites her lip and shakes her head. "Peace, I suppose. Don't you feel his presence?"

Courtenay. My emotional barriers dissolve. Yes. I sense the bond now—ever so frail. Only dark silence flows across it. "Take me to him," I say.

"Soon." Giselle glances at Dixie again, but the woman hasn't moved. "Your life flows into his. When he dies, he will drag you with him."

"As it should be," I say. I send a gentle caress across the bond but get no response.

The woman sighs. "If you were stronger—much more so—you could perhaps heal him."

"I'm not. So we die together. Is that so horrible?"

"Your children deserve a chance to live."

Yes. They complicate life's story, don't they? But I shake my head. "All we have left is each other. Take me to him."

Dixie lifts her head. Her eyes drip impatience, but the woman says nothing.

"All right," Giselle says to Dixie. Then she turns to me, takes my hand, and urges me out of the room and down the long corridor. Halfway back, she switches into lecture mode. "Near the end of World War Two, a biological weapon killed almost everyone on Eilean nan Sìthean. The children of those who survived were no longer human."

"Courtenay and me."

"He's Daoine-Sìth. You're at least part human." Close to the great room, the woman presses her hand against one of the old oak doors. After a moment, it swings open, revealing a modern-looking lab. She waves me inside.

Giselle walks to the other side of the room and presses her hand against a cabinet that has one of those biological hazard markers on it. When the door swings open, she points to a canister inside. "This is a sample of what the Daoine-Sìth call Uisge Dubh— the Black Water. They use it—in emergencies—to heal."

The woman raises a hand to her throat. To a small heart on a silver chain. Smaller than the one Mamochka gave me. When she touches it, a voice inside my head whispers, "I'm sorry my dear sister, but your sweet Annushka has no other hope."

After a moment of indecision, Giselle hands me the canister. "Take it back to the cottage," she says. "Drink it. All of it." She leads me out into the hallway. We walk together to the outer doors. She stops, but it's clear that she wants me to continue. So I wait.

The woman frowns at me. I hear her whispered thoughts inside my head, but nothing as clear as before. "Will it kill me?" I say.

She pulls me into a tight hug—something she's never done before. "Probably," she says. "I hope not." She eases away from me. "Anastasie, you're a hybrid. A result of genetic manipulation."

The woman sighs, then begins pacing. "We started with a human embryo and spliced in specific Daoine-Sìth genes." Her hand wanders up to the heart at her throat. The voice in my head whispers, "Oh, my dear Iseabail, what a mess we've made." Aloud, she says, "You may survive. I don't know."

Her eyes wander for a moment. Then she sighs. "The heart your mother gave you may be important to your survival. It dates back to a time when the last of the Daoine-Sìth interbred with mankind. In theory, it means that your ancestors were not entirely human." She presses a hand against the wall, turns, and walks away.

I sit on the bench—the one that bathed in sunlight most of the long summer days. I rub a hand across the wood, remembering my times with Courtenay, waiting here for the old oak doors to open. Even with the drugs and withdrawal, my life then was one of joyous physical activity.

I push myself to my feet and walk down the cobblestone pathway to the entrance to our meadow. Dixie's meadow, I suppose, though I rarely saw her there. Flowers and butterflies still greet me, though the scents and colors have faded to gray.

Before entering our cottage, I rest my hand on the door latch and breathe. Just breathe. Before I see my bondmate again. Before I allow myself to feel pain again. Or to give up before I begin.

Finally, I lean against the door. Till it swings open. Then shuffle across the floor to our bedroom. My bondmate isn't there. I walk across the room, pick up Courtenay's severed braid, and return to the bed, out of breath. I lie back on the mattress and close my eyes.

I dare not risk sleep, though. So I push myself upright, return her braid, and stagger out of the cottage and back across the meadow. I lean against one of the arches till my racing heart slows. Then I sit on a bench a little farther down the path.

I find Courtenay lying on her moss bed, mostly covered by the plant. Though her chest doesn't move, I sense her frail life as a gentle whisper across the bond. I lean over her, close enough to kiss. No áed flows at our touch. Nothing from me to her.

My eyes drift closed and then open again. Courtenay. Yeah. Him —though I keep slipping back to her. Not that my bondmate ever cared about gender. I should, though.

I sit beside my love and slide close, then hold up the canister. The Black Water—Courtenay said nothing at all about it, though he shared what he knew of his people's history. Does it matter? Death lies close enough now for me to smell the lilies at my funeral.

I grab the cap and twist. Hard. But it doesn't move. Hysterical laughter flows up out of my gut. "Yeah," I say. "We gave her the cure, but she couldn't get the child-proof cap off the bottle. So they both died."

Then I notice the safety latch. Duh. With a bio-hazard symbol on the side of the container, one might expect something like that. Still, Giselle should probably have pointed it out. Anyway, I get the lid off the canister.

No odor as far as I can tell, though my sense of smell sucks. I take a sip. Just a few drops. No taste. Nothing. The stuff's just water. I swallow a mouthful. And another. Still nothing. I drink the rest, or at least most of it. Then set the canister on a flat rock.

Fire explodes inside me. I roll to the side and puke. Again and again. None of the water comes back out, though. Not a single drop. I lie back in agony and close my eyes. Darkness sweeps me away.

Chapter Twenty-Five

A pulsing black star arcs across the sky, then disappears in a blinding flash and overwhelming heat. Hair, skin, and flesh melt away. My body slumps across Courtenay. Breathing slows, then stops, but my heart pounds raging madness.

Smoke rises in a column and spreads across the deep blue of early morning. Humans and Fair Folk mingle their ashes in the clouds. Their dust settles over the barren landscape and mixes with the sea water that flows into the crater left by the explosion.

Black liquid surges around me—carrying with it bacteria from a biological weapon, the remains of frail humans incinerated by the blast, and particles of the bones of Fair Folk long dead—all burning away my life. My body slips beneath the murky water.

Sights and sounds flood my soul—a father with his daughter, sitting in a meadow beside the Daoine-Sìth burial mounds—an elder of the gentle race pleading with the humans not to kill her children —a soldier on leave, frowning at the sky—a little boy, playing with a frog.

Days pass. They stretch into eons as hundreds share their untimely deaths with me. I cling in terror to my own memories, lest I be swept away. Brit. Courtenay. Mamochka. Even the trauma of Kyrill's abuse helps me endure. Till at last the storm subsides, and I stand on the edge of a crater lake surrounded by majestic pines. Not a ripple disturbs the black surface.

Daoine-Sìth survive not long the death of a bondmate. Most of us find our way down to the sea and surrender to the deep. Though the halfling spawn of Human and Fair Folk, I stand on the rocky shore of Còir-Bhreith, the birthright of the Daoine-Sìth. I claim the Black Water as my own, if only for my death. Into its depths I plunge.

Còir-Bhreith holds the promise of peace. One day, a human war will unleash the Black Water—and death—upon the world. I shudder at a fleeting vision of the final conflict. Only my people—the Daoine-Sìth—will survive. Yes. My people.

The survivors of the initial blast were all descended from a single woman. Not human, but bean-sìthe. Fair Folk. She'd married William Kirkpatrick and given him fae daughters.

One of his granddaughters was in London when the bomb struck Eilean nan Sìthean. With her was her three-year-old daughter—my great-grandmother. I was able to bond with Courtenay—and survive the Black Water—not because of any of Giselle's gene splices, but because I'm a direct mother-to-daughter descendant of a Daoine-Sìth woman. I was never human.

Eilean nan Sìthean fades into darkness. Awareness returns, and with it pain. In the twilight of the solarium I raise my hands and flex delicate fingers in agony. The silver chain in my hand—the heart my mother gave me—still glows with the dealan that would have swept me away had I been entirely human.

The heart's not silver. Not pewter. But a metal unknown to the humans who drove the Daoine-Sìth from their first homeland. My people call it àeileanì. We brought tonnes of the precious metal with us to Eilean nan Sìthean. We buried it with our dead. We passed it down to our children's children. It's our life blood. And why I'm no longer human. Me. Anya.

I hold up my hand as the pain recedes. The flesh mends even as I watch. Yes. The Black Water. But nausea constricts my chest and throat. Cramps knot my abdomen. Beads of black liquid flow down my face and drip on the moss bed. Healing isn't always pleasant.

Nor are the visions that haunt me now. I press both hands against my head, hoping to dislodge them, to forget the memories of the dead, to no longer hear their screams or feel their pain. My hands brush against elfin ears—now long and slender. One twitches.

Eilidh—or at least the memory of the young Daoine-Sìth who drowned herself in the Black Water—she insists that I must eat.

Immediately. Or risk an unpleasant death. I roll away from Courtenay and sit up, but wait till the world stops spinning before I stand.

Coirce—Eilidh's memory provides a name for the plant next to our mossy bed. Or at least its scent. Oatmeal. Pecans. Honey. Saliva runs in my mouth. I turn my head away and puke till only bile remains. A frantic hunger overtakes me then. I tear off one of the saucer-shaped pods and stuff the thing into my mouth. Whole. Hope they're not poisonous.

Sùbh-craoibhe—another scent from Eilidh's memory. I pull a fist-sized fruit from the plant and bite into it. Juice from the hollow center runs down my chin. The sticky fluid tastes like blueberry or maybe raspberry. No seeds.

After a few more coirce pods, I wander back to Courtenay. The bond pulses with my heartbeat now. Perhaps hers as well. Slow. Peaceful. Strong.

I kiss my bondmate's lips. Flickering blue shadows—áed—the fire of our love.

Dealan—the cinnamon fire between bondmates.

Yes. I run gentle fingers down Courtenay's chest, leaving a soft azure glow.

Dealan—the pulsing warmth within a Daoine-Sìth.

I remember. A well-spring of energy, surging even now in me.

Dealan—the healing touch of a mother for her child or bondmate.

Yes. I've mended both heartbreak and fractured bones. I remember how.

Dealan—the lightning strike of a Daoine-Sìth warrior.

I killed a direwolf with a single bolt from my hand. My hand.

"No. Not me," I whisper to the shadows. "I'm Anya." My body trembles. The air around me vibrates with energy. My hand slides away from Courtenay. I'm a danger to her now.

Uisge Dubh—Eilidh's memory again. Yes. The Black Water. I find the canister and swallow the few mouthfuls that remain. The liquid burns so hot that I grab another sùbh-craoibhe and soothe my mouth with its gentle coolness.

I return to Courtenay and press my hand against her chest. The bond sparkles—diamond dust floating in a sunbeam. So fragile. A whisper of dealan sends tiny sparks dashing along that lifeline. It's not enough, though. And I dare not use more.

Màthair—Eilidh's mother healed her once. That memory didn't help her dying bondmate.

Màthair-àil—First Mother—the generation of human females that survived the plague could sometimes heal their children and grandchildren. No help there, either.

Hundreds of Fair Folk were buried in the mounds on Eilean nan Sìthean. Their faded memories but ghostly shadows. Indistinct. Yet their gentle elders spoke tenderness, affection, and compassion to those in need of healing, whether friend or foe.

Ìosa—not a word from the Daoine-Sìth, but a person. Such an ancient people. So strange to the humans who killed them. Yet they worshiped a most merciful God.

Nì mi sìth, the heart says. I'll make peace. Daoine-Sìth—the people of peace. Slaughtered by humans the first time. Reborn now, but under military quarantine by humans who kill without mercy any who stray from Eilean nan Sìthean.

I take Courtenay's hands in mine and plead with my bondmate to return. Peace, joy, love, and mercy—I beg Mrs. Andrews' God to answer me. My heart bleeds across the bond—till the sun rises and sets again. Till I collapse across my bondmate.

Chapter Twenty-Six

Just one possibility remains open to me. I see that now. In the early morning, I walk back along the cobblestone trail to the cherry grove. Moonlight guides me to the boulder where I waited for my mother. She's not coming, though I'm sure of what she would say—don't my precious Annushka. Please don't.

Death. Mine. Courtenay's. Our children's. I can't heal my bond-mate, but neither will I let him die. I run a hand across the cold granite before sitting. The shattered memories cluttering my mind are just ancient black and white snapshots. What were they thinking at the moment of their death? Ordinary things, mostly. Till the light and the heat and the pain overwhelmed everything else.

Yet a few—even in their agony—cared more about their loved ones than about their own misery. They comfort me now. Fragments of other lives show me what I must do, though the drawing's not complete. The paint's been spilled and drips down the canvas.

To save Courtenay, I must lose him. To keep him from giving himself to the sea, he must not remember me. Even then, the price of his life is dear. Not only must I forget him, but much of who I am will vanish as well.

So I wait in the moonlight. Till the horizon glows a dark red. Then I walk back to my bondmate and sit on the moss bed next to my love. One last time, I run a hand down his arm, inhale deep of the cinnamon, and smile at the blue sparks that fall from my fingertips.

Nì mi sìth, Mamochka's heart says. I'll make peace. I hold my mother's precious gift in my hands and pray for Courtenay. For Remie and Taylor. Then I push as much dealan—and as much of myself—into the metal as I dare. My time with Courtenay, our friendship, our bonding, our children—I yield them all to the void. But I must still find my way out. Or all will be in vain.

That's what the memories tell me. What becomes of me, then? They don't say. Perhaps they don't know. Just that I must leave. Now. My body's already changing. So I kiss my love goodbye and push myself to my feet.

I stumble across the meadow and down the cobblestone pathway toward the cherry grove again. And the statue of Mamochka. Forever—in my dreams—I waited for her in this garden, wandering among the pink and white flowers. She never came for me. I've carried that pain for years.

Yet it wasn't my mother who abandoned me—whether here or when Papa murdered her. I'm the one who shifted to another place and left her desolate. My gaze drifts back down the path—toward Courtenay and our children. Yes. My fault. But my bondmate won't grieve if he doesn't remember me. Won't give himself to the sea. So I abandon him. And my children. As I did my mother.

I run a hand across my itching breasts. No need to look down— my body's returning to its pre-bond form. I'm inches taller than I was an hour ago. A muscle in my leg cramps. Though I'm free of drugs, the clouds of withdrawal stretch across my horizon. Near me, the sky darkens.

Stillness in my head now—the memories lie dormant. I rub a weary arm across my forehead, then down the front of my jersey in a futile attempt to ease the pain.

Ben slaps my back. Jackson does as well. Finally, Dylan throws an arm around my shoulder and pulls me close. "Awesome shot," he says.

Dylan—a tremor runs through my exhausted muscles in answer to his touch. "Yeah. Guess so."

"No. Seriously, dude. You won us the match."

I glance up to see if the boy's joking, but his brown eyes hold only tenderness. I kiss him on the lips, though our friends are watching. Somewhere—in another place—I owed him a sweetheart's goodbye.

The boy's face turns a bright red, but his smile grows wide. "A practical joke—right? You sure got me on that one." He slaps me on the shoulder before wandering back toward his motorcycle. "See you in a few minutes."

A young woman steps out of the crowd and stops in front of me. She's tall and thin. Beautiful, actually. With an awesome watercolor tattoo on one cheek. "I'm Jazmine Lamont," she says. "Your new CASA volunteer. Court Appointed Special Advocate."

My gaze wanders back to Dylan. He smiles at me and waves. Does the boy know that I'm Anya and not Anatoli? I turn back to the woman, not sure what to say.

"You're Anna Gilyova, right?" Her smile assures me that all is well in our world. So I nod.

"Can we talk?" she says. "I'll give you a ride back to the Andrews' place."

Not my foster home. She knows that I'm playing soccer as a boy. So the court does as well. My foster parents don't want me back. I close my eyes for a moment. The end has been coming since my body started changing.

"All right," I say. Like I have any other choices. "But I'm supposed to take a motorcycle ride." My gaze wanders back to Dylan on his bike. A tall boy stands close by him, helmet in hand. Anatoli. Me. "Never mind," I say as the boys ride off together.

Ms. Lamont leads me to her car—a rusty old Chevy. Guess a decent ride isn't required to be a CASA volunteer. I smile at the woman and slide into the passenger seat.

We drive the few minutes it takes to get to one of the restaurants in Zelienople. She leads me inside and to a booth in the back corner. "Something to eat?" she says. "My treat."

"Coffee would be great. Thanks."

After the waitress brings our drinks, Ms. Lamont slides a billfold out of her purse. She shows me her CASA ID and a Pennsylvania Drivers License. After she puts those away, she pulls out a notepad. "Okay," she says. "The Randalls told your caseworker that you were playing soccer as a boy. For that reason—and due to your recent physical issues—they no longer wish to be your foster parents."

No surprise there. My body changes, and everybody freaks.

"I read the doctor's report. And spoke with the psychologist you saw for your evaluation. Your caseworker and I agree to your staying with the Andrews family on a temporary basis. If you're willing. And if the family can provide you with your own bedroom."

My brain refuses to process her statement. Or its implications. Yeah—of course the Randalls would kick me out. But family services let me stay with Brit and her mom? Not likely. I nod. And grin. But that's all I can manage.

A muscle in my leg twitches. My stomach rumbles. I have to set my coffee on the table because my hand is shaking so much. My eyes keep wandering back to Ms. Lamont's face. Yeah, she's pretty. I get that. I'm attracted to some girls. But this woman's probably nineteen or twenty—a little old for me. Still, my body thinks we're lovers.

My face warms. I turn my gaze away. Yeah—twenty years old, at the most. Do they let you be a CASA volunteer that young? But she showed me her ID. She's probably legit. The woman smiles and leans toward me. "You were born in Canada?" she says.

No. "I grew up in Erie," I say, though my memory suddenly isn't sure of my birthplace.

The woman shrugs and smiles at me. Like she knows that's not right.

I shake my head at her. "I've been in foster care since my mother died." My eyes do a slow blink. What happened to Mamochka? I waited, wandering through the cherry trees, looking for her. No. Not her. My mother. I left her.

Kyrill stabbed Mamochka. Didn't he? I stare at the table in front of me. Till Ms. Lamont rests her hand on mine. "It's okay," she says. "You'll remember what matters when the time comes."

My eyes meet hers then. "Can the Andrews family adopt me?"

"You'll have a forever family soon," she says and squeezes my hand. "Days. Perhaps weeks. Not longer." The woman digs into her purse and pulls out a small white box. "I'm not sure why this was kept from you, but Courtenay and I want you to have possession of it."

"Courtenay?" Not even sure who that is.

"Courtenay Dubois," the woman says. "Your new caseworker. He lost his wife recently, so he can't meet yet. But he wanted to be sure that you got your necklace back right away."

Jewelry. I haven't worn any in months. Not since I started playing soccer as Anatoli. A sigh lifts my shoulders. I don't care that much about girly stuff. But I open the box. Inside, between layers of cotton padding, lies a silver heart on a fine chain. It's been polished till the surface shines with an inner light. Deep within the metal glows a Saint Andrew's cross in a pastel blue. The heart appears to be etched with some foreign language.

Mamochka gave the pendant to me for Christmas when I was young. How could I forget? And when did they take it from me? When she was murdered?

No. My mother gave the heart to me while in Canada, just before I wandered the cherry grove.

No. My twin sister returned the heart a year ago.

Except that I don't have a sister.

Anastasie gave the heart to me.

No. I'm Anastasie.

I press both hands to my head, hoping to keep from drowning in the tsunami of memory fragments.

"Thank you," I say. The pendant is clearly mine. So I clasp the chain around my neck and refuse to remember anything more. But the heat that flows into me draws old memories to the surface. Fragments of pain and death flood me.

Ms. Lamont slides out of the booth. "Unless you have questions, we're finished. The Andrews will need to fill out some paperwork, but I think you're ready. You do want to stay with them?"

"Yes, ma'am." A muscle in my arm twitches. My legs shake like twisted rubber bands.

On the ride back to New Brighton, Ms. Lamont asks me how I'm coping with the changes.

"My body's fine," I say. It's my mind that bothers me.

After the woman pulls into the driveway at the Andrews home, she hands me a business card. "If you have any issues—any at all—

feel free to contact me. Treatment decisions are between you and your doctors, but I need to know what you decide."

I stand on the porch and watch till the car's gone. I'm finally home. Won't it be easier for family services to let me stay with the Andrews forever than to move me to another placement? Why spend any more time on my case, if they don't have to? They certainly have enough others.

As soon as I step inside, Brit comes running down the stairs. "Annushka! What are you doing here? You're gonna get Ma and me in trouble."

I hold out Ms. Lamont's business card. "My new CASA volunteer says I can stay with you."

Brit scowls at the card and shakes her head. "What about the No Contact Order the court issued last week?"

My shoulders rise in a helpless shrug. "I don't know. Maybe your mom should call Ms. Lamont."

My bestie pulls me into an awesome hug. "Well, I guess it don't matter. Anyway, I'm glad you're here." Then a grin blossoms on her face. "Since you are, let's catch up on the photos. Okay?"

"Sure." I follow her up the stairs and down the hallway to the work room. Hours pass as I model vintage clothes and then help Brit post the best of the pictures on their website. I am so gonna love being her sister.

Chapter Twenty-Seven

Seriously—the best sleep is always that last little bit of coasting before I get up. While the pleasant dreams linger. A yawn brings a smile to my face. I stretch my arms above my head. Brit lies close beside me. She groans and rolls over. The bed squeaks a good morning to both of us.

Mrs. Andrews taps on the door, walks across the room, and sits next to Brit. She promised Ms. Lamont that I'd have my own bedroom. I do. But we never told anybody that I'd actually sleep there. Brit and I would rather not be alone all night. And our mom doesn't care if her daughters snuggle. Not like we're gonna have sex. 'Cause we're sisters, you perv.

Mrs. Andrews leans down and brushes ginger hair away from my eyes. "We have a guest," she says. "Get dressed and come down to the kitchen. All right, girls?"

"Yes, Mamochka." My need for a mother surges again. This has gotta work out.

"All right, Ma." Brit stands. She stretches again as her mother turns to go.

Twenty after six. Who knocks on somebody's door this early? I pull the drapes open. In the driveway sits a black Escalade. Déjà vu hits me hard then—a vision of a US marshal sitting at the kitchen table. A blond man of Russian extraction, claiming to be my father. Except that mine's in a prison near Edinboro.

Or is he? Chaotic glimpses of the past swirled through the night, disturbing my sleep. Some of my memories seem but painted nesting dolls—layers of fantasy meant to hide the truth. Lies. Like Kyrill Mikhailovich Gilyov. Perhaps even Mamochka.

I press my face against the window and sigh. Images of what my father did to my mother no longer haunt me. Nor fear of his abuse. I'll never see the man again. If he ever existed.

I jump when someone touches me. It's only Brit, though. "Better hurry," she says.

My bestie. Yeah. She's real. I rush down the hallway to my bedroom to grab my clothes. I do everything in my room except sleep there. When I'm dressed, I follow my bestie downstairs to the kitchen.

A blond-haired man in a dark blue jacket sits at the table, holding a coffee cup with both hands. Down his sleeve runs US MARSHAL. Well that sucks. Here to enforce the No Contact Order. I'm going to a new placement. Already. Or a detention center.

Mrs. Andrews waves me toward my usual seat. Then she brings bacon, eggs, and toast to the table. She says grace, but I guess only Brit and I are eating breakfast.

US marshal. Black SUV. My hand wanders up to the heart at my throat—my precious gift from Mamochka. Or my mother in Canada. The stranger nods—just a slight bobbing of his head. My necklace means something to him. Not like I stole the thing, though.

After Brit and I finish, I rinse the plates and silverware and find room for them in the dishwasher. Then, I sit down again. Like the dude's gonna watch me eat breakfast and then leave. Yeah. I expect the Spanish Inquisition. The cuckoo clock in the hallway squawks agreement.

A tremor shakes my arm. Let the questions begin. But the man just smiles and nods. "I'm Inspector Ilya Koshkin," he says. Then he pulls a stack of papers out of his briefcase. "Your birth name was Ruairi Anna Gilchrist?"

His statement cracks several of the outer shells, but I shake my head. "Anna Gilyova," I say, though the distant shadows of memories name me a liar. Ruairi's a boy's name. And Russian middle names are derived from the father's given name. My father was Kyrill. I'm a girl. That makes my middle name Kyrillovna. And the feminine form of my father's surname is Gilyova.

But what if Kyrill never existed? Why would I be Anna Gilyova? My mother was Scottish. Gilchrist might be Scottish.

"Do you have a copy of your birth certificate?" he says. In his eyes, I see compassion. But he's certain I've got my name wrong.

"No, sir." Kyrill burned mine a couple of days before he killed Mamochka.

Kyrill. No.

I wandered through the cherry grove, waiting for my mother. My body shifted somewhere else, leaving her behind. A new family took me in—a father named Kyrill Mikhailovich Gilyov, and a mother named Iseabail Gilyova. Anna Kyrillovna Gilyova. Me. Never Ruairi. No. Not him. My body was never male.

Tenderness and concern both shine from the man's face. Like he has good news that's gonna hurt.

"Doesn't family services have my birth certificate?" I say. They know my name.

The dude slides an open Canadian Passport across the table. Ruairi Anna Gilchrist. Of course. That's what the man said. Parents Iseabail/Kaid. Okay. Place of birth Eilean nan Sìthean. Scotland. Island of the Fairie Mounds. The place Courtenay was born.

Courtenay.

Dixie.

Jazmine.

I close my eyes as a hundred painful deaths sweep across me. My body sways. I grab the table with both hands to keep from drowning. I breathe deep till the moment passes.

The photo in the passport shows a pink-eyed, white-haired Daoine-Sìth child. I'm not a hybrid. Not any more human than Courtenay was. Ruairi Anna Gilchrist. My bondmate said they gave their children both a masculine and a feminine name.

My eyes wander away from Mr. Koshkin. And meet Brit's intense gaze. She knows that everything the marshal said is true. Everything. And something else. She knows that she's gonna lose me. Soon.

The marshal returns his papers to his briefcase and then smiles at me. "I understand that this may be a bit overwhelming. I'll come back next week, and we can review your case." His face grows serious—like a father's might be when saying goodbye to his daughter. "I'll try to answer any questions you may have then."

After he leaves, I rush up the stairs to Brit's room. The man walks out to the black Escalade and drives away. Just like that.

Brit slides an arm around my waist and presses her face close to mine. "I love you," she says. "Even though you're not my Annushka."

"Huh?" My head swivels around. Like an owl's. Yeah. Like that.

"Mrs. Randall called last night. She wanted to know if she could pick up Anya's watercolors. Then she put Anya on the phone to explain where they were. My Anya. Not you."

Two of me? Well that sucks. "How?" Like she'll know what I mean.

She grins like a bean-sìthe on a death watch. "I hear things sometimes. Like the voice in my head that tells me you belong to her. That she loves you even more than I do. And she wants you back."

"She?"

"Her name's Brit. 'Cause she didn't like the name her parents gave her. Like me."

Another Brit. Glad I'm not the only one who's crazy. "I love you," I say and kiss my bestie on the cheek. Dealan surges around me when I do. The storm approaches. Brit may be right.

I run down the hallway to the work room and sift through my stuff there. Till I find my oriental landscape. The other Anya's, I suppose. So I set it aside and pull out a clean piece of paper.

Doing watercolors in a rush is never the best idea. But I want to leave my bestie—this one—a memory. And—wherever I'm going—it's soon. Way too soon for me.

So I sharpen a pencil and sketch the cherry grove. I remember it now. As it really is. Without the steel and glass canopy. With a dusting of snow on the blossoms. Pink and lilac and cream. Dark brown. A cold haze above the barren hills. Eilean nan Sìthean in winter. My childhood home. Yeah. Mine.

An hour passes while I paint—ever so careful with the brush and the drops and—especially—the acrylics. But, yeah, I finish the thing without ruining it. Then I set it aside to dry.

Lightning strikes somewhere in the distance. The lights go out. The power's out, but dealan flows into me now. Perhaps—just perhaps—there's time for a second painting.

So I pencil in the lines for Anya. The one who's not sure of her body. The one who's just a little bit crazy from the whirlwind that drives her along. Yeah. Me. Ginger hair, wild from dealan—or maybe just static. Vintage gown flowing, with a couple of small tears. And a mud stain.

The sky drips as I rush to paint it. Orange and blue run together, down across the—yeah the stylized coirce pods. I finish just as Brit rushes into the room. "Now," she says. Yes. Now. Mamochka's heart burns against my chest. It lights the room.

Static crackles through the air. Brit's long hair floats up in a cloud around her head and shoulders. I pull her into a tight hug. "Goodbye," I whisper.

A cold wind and bleak sunshine welcome me home. The cries of seagulls float on the salt air. I pull Brit closer and stroke the girl's hair. Blonde hair. In a braid.

A few more minutes pass before she eases away from me. Not Brit. Brìghde—my best friend when I was a little kid. Before I shifted away. And abandoned her.

To be fair—not Brìghde either. She never liked that name. Peadar.

Peadar Brìghde Aindréas. Though convention says golds use their feminine middle name, Peadar never wanted to be called Brìghde. Not even as a wee bànag with white hair and pink eyes. Which is when Daoine-Sìth children are encouraged to try out both of their names.

A sigh lifts my shoulders. Yeah. Like me. Ruairi Anna Gilchrist— who still doesn't want to be called Ruairi, though my hair's definitely red now. I grab a strand, eye it carefully, and then sigh again. Yeah, red.

"I appreciate the welcome, Peadar, but how did you end up in a hug with me?"

A grin spreads across her pretty face. "Brit and I were close," is all the girl will say.

Chapter Twenty-Eight

Eilean nan Sìthean—I drink deep of the island's beauty. "I'm home, Peadar," I say. "Forever."

My bestie's face glows. "I was headed up to Am Bàrr," she says. "You want to go?" Her eyes hold the same fear that I've seen there too many times. In a land where only reds can bond, what happens to someone whose body never gets past being gold?

"Sure," I say, and hug her again. Yeah. Her body and my gender. Frozen in time.

Peadar leads, though we both know the way. I smile at my bestie as she takes my hand. A gold's never supposed to wander about alone. I'm the red. I should lead, they'd say. Boys should protect girls. Boys are stronger and more agile. Golds are too frail. I grin at her again.

My bestie stops. She eyes me for a moment, not quite smiling or frowning. But totally serious. "Please call me Brit now," she says.

A chill runs through me. Brit—Bridgitte Peta Andrews. Peadar Brìghde Aindréas. "That was you?" I say. Like she'll know what I'm talking about.

Surprise touches Peadar's face, something I've not often seen there. After a moment, she shakes her head. "No. At least I don't think so. For a while, we shared the same eyes. And the same heart for you. I want that now—to be Brit for you."

The old cobblestone pathway meanders between rocks and trees, winding its way uphill to Am Bàrr. And the most spectacular views on the island. "Thank you," I say. "And I'm sorry that I didn't pay more attention to her. Or you. We were best friends."

Brit—suddenly timid—runs on ahead. Around the peak—well, hilltop, really. I stand there, taking in the trees and the ocean and the distant islands. And, yes, the old American aircraft carrier that guards our shores. Flipping them the bird would kinda spoil the moment. So I save my dislike for later.

We've been under a strict military quarantine since World War Two—they're that afraid of the Daoine-Sìth. The human Outsiders kill anyone who tries to leave our island. Sometimes even people in small boats, fishing off our shores.

When Peadar comes close enough again, I mouth, "I love you." She frowns. But someday she'll let me say that aloud without getting upset

"I see things, sometimes," she says. "Like you and Brit." Her eyes grow sad, but she doesn't mention Courtenay. Is it wrong that I miss Brit more than my bondmate?

I scan the treetops again before sitting on the hillside facing the Gilchrist farm. My old home. Where I lived with Dad and Mom and seven siblings. Till my parents died, and I went to stay with Peadar's family.

I perch on a flat rock on the hillside. My bestie scoots in close beside me. We sit the way we used to—when we were just two kids with long golden braids, feeling alone in a world where girls become teenage boys before a kiss triggers puberty, and their bodies become male or female.

An hour passes in perfect contentment. Maybe two. While the cold wind blows across our backs, and the sky darkens. Winter approaches. Weather here can be brutal. And we don't have a heated solarium to keep us warm.

"I see things, sometimes," Brit says again. "that nobody else does."

"Like what?" I say, though the hairs on the back of my neck crawl.

"You don't see it," she says. Suddenly, she finds something interesting in her lap.

My hand moves to the heart at my throat. The air grows tense around me. "Where?"

My bestie points down into the valley, toward the Brùn family tavern. "There's a bird there. I see its dealan." She shakes her head. "Not like a seagull. This one carries its eggs with it."

My eyesight is outstanding, but even squinting, I see nothing. Not like I can see a person's dealan, anyhow. And, whoever heard of a bird having any?

"She's gonna drop her eggs!" Brit stands just as an explosion echoes across the island. Smoke rises from the old tavern. In the distance, people run around like crazy ants. My bestie waves her arms and starts running.

"Wait!" As soon as I can catch up, I grab her arm. "Where's the bird? Where is it? Where?" What else is the thing gonna bomb?

Brit's mouth works for a moment, but nothing comes out. Then she dips behind me and covers my eyes with her hands. Yeah. Like wouldn't pointing be better? I can't see anything with my eyes covered.

Except that—in the sky floats a jumble of pulsing lines. Almost like a network of interconnected bonds. Yeah. Like that. Lots of parts talking to each other over sparkling threads. In the shape of a bird. In the sky. Coming this way.

"Targets acquired," the bird says to itself. Or maybe to someone on the ground. Far away. Like on an aircraft carrier. The network flashes pictures of the old Fearghas warehouse. Then video of the approach to Am Bàrr. Soon, the drone will be right over us.

My heart stutters, but I can't take my eyes away. Can't run. Can't hide. Can't move.

A memory floats up out of my past then—one of the ancient Daoine-Sìth warriors. A way to gather enough dealan to stop an airplane. Look, I don't want any superpowers, okay? I'm a sixteen-year-old intersex elfin girl. That's enough, ain't it?

Am I willing to die to kill the thing and save the Fearghas family? Yeah. Why not? I failed at dying last time. Maybe I can do better now.

"Arm AGM-114s," the bird says, as though our deaths won't matter at all.

Jazmine cut my life short. And Dixie. I gave all I had to Courtenay. Then lost her. I'm home now. I can live as long as anyone else on this island. If I get behind a rock somewhere. Instead of pretending to be some ancient elfin warrior. Because dead people remember stuff. In my head.

"I love you, Brit," I say. Yeah. I'd die for her. Then I hold up one hand in front of me. Like that's gonna stop a huge military aircraft. As the UAV passes overhead, missiles fire. Lightning jumps between me and the airplane. Between me and the missiles. Again. And again. And again. If there were electricity on Eilean nan Sithean, the lights would be out now.

All of the deaths that the Black Water left me—all of their turmoil rides the glowing ashes drifting down out of the sky. Again. At least nobody new had to die.

Daoine-Sith—the People of Peace. Though it sometimes works, violence is rarely justified. Hot ash rains down on me. My body—drained of dealan—and of life itself—slumps to the ground. The darkness of night washes over my soul as Brit holds me.

Chapter Twenty-Nine

Puffy white clouds float across the late afternoon sky. Gulls dance high above us. Somewhere close by, a lamb bleats for its mother. I breathe deep of the pines and flowers and the cold sea breeze. It is so good to be back on Eilean nan Sìthean.

Echoes of massive explosions reverberate within me still, somewhere in the back of my head. I sit up in a panic, but my bestie looks happy enough. "You okay?" I ask her.

"I can't see," she says. "The lightning was brighter than the sun, and I watched. You killed the bird and all of her eggs. Can you take me home? I want to find out if anyone was hurt."

Blind. My fault. Nice. I try to stand, but something isn't working right. My left hand still clutches the heart, but there's no flesh on the bones. My right— My right arm's missing. My clothes are gone—burned away. Charred flesh runs all the way down my side. My right leg ends in a blackened stump. Why am I not screaming in pain?

"No one else was injured," a voice says. A horse steps into view —Eachann—the lord of all the steeds on Eilean nan Sìthean. His wet coat shifts between dark green and a glossy black. Beside him stands a woman, her golden hair dripping wet. Like she was just swimming. Instead of riding to the top of Am Bàrr.

"You wield great power," she says, "but you may wish to learn better control."

I laugh. Wild and free. I just got cremated, and she's gonna lecture me? "I'm dying, lady. There won't be a next time."

She pats Eachann on the neck and steps closer. "Would you not rather be healed?"

Like anybody can. But my gaze wanders over to Brit. "Would you help her first? She's blind now."

The lady glances toward my bestie. Then her shoulders rise in a careless shrug. "No," is all she says.

Bitch. "All right," I say.

Venora's the prettiest woman on Eilean nan Sìthean—so they say. She hangs out with Eachann, who is probably a kelpie. Her hair always drips with sea water. Some suspect her of being truly fae. Yet she always seems to help. Though reluctantly. Fine.

Her dealan raises the hair on the back of my neck as she steps close. The woman sits on the ground beside me and runs her fingertips over my charred flesh. "Close your eyes," she says. "Your sight will only distract you."

Yeah. Right. But I shut my eyes. I don't need to see the ashes that she's brushing away.

She runs fingertips across my arm. My abdomen. My leg. "You've burned almost a third of your mass," she says. "You'll have to work with what remains."

The woman presses a hand to my forehead then. "Concentrate. A few years ago, you were òr. Blue eyes, golden braid—gentle girl, at home she stays."

Yeah. Enough with the nursery rhymes. Okay? A sigh manages to work its way up out of my gut.

"You're òr again," she says. "For now. Embrace any pleasant memories you have from those years."

I'm burned to a crisp, and she thinks she can talk me into being healed? Yeah, I had a great time as a gold. It was my body changes that led to emotional issues. Given a choice, I'd rather be that petite blonde than a tall and muscular redhead. Any day, lady.

But wishing ain't gonna fix things. And she doesn't appear to be doing anything to help. So I open my eyes in frustration. Then gasp. I'm sitting in a pile of burned goo, but my leg, my abdomen, my hands are all fine. I push myself to my feet. My body's restored. Naked. But healthy.

Okay, so I'm six inches shorter than I was. And I probably have blonde hair and blue eyes. "Will you heal Peadar now? Please?"

"I can't," she says and walks back to Eachann.

"Why not?"

She smiles and shakes her head. "You'll have to find his mother or bond with him. I can only help my own children and bondmate."

"You just healed me."

"No. I talked you into regenerating."

For a moment, my brain refuses to process her words. Then my eyes flick over to Eachann. Kelpie. And back to her. Selkie. Beings that can change shape. I shake my head and step back. "Daoine-Sìth don't regenerate."

The lady's eyes grow suddenly weary. She pulls herself up on to Eachann's back. "True," she says. "But Daoine-Sìth who give themselves to the sea become Daoine-Mara." The woman nods farewell. Eachann turns and walks away.

Daoine-Sìth—people of peace. Daoine-Mara—people of the sea. As in mermaid. Selkie. Kelpie. "I've never been in the ocean," I say. A bean-sìthe becoming a mermaid after drowning. That old myth. Though I would have given myself to the sea after losing Courtenay, it would have meant my death. Wasn't that the point?

I scrape around in the ashes, but only small fragments remain of my clothing. So I turn to Brit. "Can I borrow your cloak?" I say. "My clothes are gone."

She slips off her coat and hands it to me. "You don't have to bond with me," she says.

"Yes, I do. It's my fault that you're blind."

"No. I could have closed my eyes and looked away. I'm not even ruadh yet. And what happens if you turn out to be the male after we bond?"

My bestie can't see, but she's more afraid of becoming a woman than of remaining blind. Do I fear becoming a man that much? Yeah. Probably. But I'd never admit it.

When my mother gave me the heart, she told me that it had been handed down from mother to daughter for three hundred years. I always thought that was because I was a gold—her daughter.

Is the heart why I became female when I bonded? A permanent daughter rather than a temporary one? I lift the heart to examine it. Could a piece of metal with a St. Andrew's cross have determined what sex I became? Would the same thing happened if Peadar Brìghde Aindréas and I bonded? I kinda hope so.

I hug my bestie and lead her down the trail toward home. The ghosts of memories follow us. An eye doctor who lost his sight—and his life—the day the rocket exploded over Eilean nan Sìthean. The Daoine-Sìth elder who inscribed Nì Mi Sìth on my heart.

Will Brit ever see again? Was I right to use violence to protect my people?

We arrive at the Aindréas homestead just as the sun sets and the breeze turns cold. The horizon turns a deep purple and crimson. Darkness creeps across the sea toward us.

I lead Brit down the hallway to our bedroom. Yeah. Still just one small bed. "You slept alone while I was gone?" Nobody does that. Not on Eilean nan Sìthean. Not when families have eight little girls that become eight teenage boys.

But she nods. Because her body's different—not ruadh yet, though it should be. And she insists on using her masculine name, though she's at least as girly as any of her sisters.

When my parents died, the Aindréas family took me in, but I shared a room with Peadar rather than their sons. Because I didn't like being called Ruairi and hated that my body was becoming ruadh —like their sons.

So the boys teased us both, and we spent our time with each other—as sisters—but separated from the other girls. For days we went back to the cherry grove and waited for my mother to return. And then one day I heard my mother's voice and blinked. When I opened my eyes again, I was with Mamochka.

The wash basin has fresh water, so I wipe myself with a cloth and then find one of my old dresses in Brit's closet. The memory of my vintage farm-girl clothes brings a smile to my face, but my own dress is simpler and just as comfy.

I wipe my bestie's face clean and help her wash her hands.

The door squeaks open. Brit's mother looks in. Joy shines from her face. "Ruairi Anna! I thought I saw you come in. Welcome home!" She sweeps me off the floor into a hug and swings me around.

"Where were you?" She takes a step back. "And you're òr again!"

Brit tugs on the woman's dress. "She almost got killed today. All right, Ma? We were up on Am Bàrr when the storm hit and that bird exploded."

The woman sets me down. Her gaze flicks from me to Brit and back again. She pulls me close and kisses my forehead. "She's right. It doesn't matter where you were. You're always welcome here." Then she sits on the bed and pats the mattress beside her. "What have you done to yourself this time, Peadar? Let me look at you."

"I'm okay, Ma. I just can't see very well."

"Peadar Brìghde Aindréas. Come over here right now."

Brit holds her hands out in front of her and shuffles across the room like some zombie. Her mother glances at me and rolls her eyes. She places both hands on Brit's head. Her face twists in concentration. My bestie's eyes go wide for a moment before her mother relaxes. "Is that better?"

Brit looks around the room and then grins. "Yeah. Thanks, Ma. I love you."

"I know, darling." she says. "Are you two hungry? There's some leftover cullen skink."

Smoked fish chowder. Soup with haddock, potatoes, and onion. I hate the stuff. Or at least I used to. But saliva runs in my mouth and my stomach growls. Right now I'd eat an entire school of fish raw. And no, I'm not a mermaid. Or a selkie. Or a kelpie. Just a hungry kid.

Brit takes my hand—like she owns me—and leads me to the kitchen. A cast iron pot sits on the old stove. My bestie grabs a mitt and lifts the lid from the stew. I rush to the cabinet and find a couple of pottery bowls.

The dining area's empty. The girls have already cleaned up after supper, so we eat in the kitchen and are careful not to make a mess. And yes, the stew is yummy. What can I say? I like fish now.

The boys are talking in the great room. The girls are in the den. So Brit and I wander back down the hallway to her room and sit on the bed. The sun's down, so the house will be dark soon enough. No electricity. No oil lamps. No candles. We can get around in darkness if we have to, but who wants a stubbed toe?

In the twilight, we change into our nightgowns. Not the nylon and chiffon of vintage négligées, but still comfy and warm. I brush my hair and work it into a loose braid. Then sit on the mattress and wait.

Brit stands next to the bed in dark silence, head down. Outside, the wind moans. Raindrops splash against the window. When my bestie looks up again, she sighs. "I want the relationship you and the other Brits had."

She kept me alive. Encouraged me. Protected me. "So do I. And more."

"Can we be sisters, then?" she says. Her eyes shine in the twilight.

I stand and hug her like I never want to let go. 'Cause I don't. "We are sisters, Brit. Forever. And we'll be more."

My bestie looks down at the floor again. Is she that afraid of bonding? Of the possibility of ending up female? No. She's more feminine than most of her sisters. But she's spent her entire life asking people to call her Peadar rather than Brìghde, and most refuse. Her only hope of that ever ending is if she becomes male after bonding.

Brit's eyes glisten in the night, but I dare not hold her now. Not till she wants. "When you're ruadh again," she says, "you can bond with anyone. Your dealan is awesome. You're smart. You're pretty. And you care about people. You won't have any trouble finding a bondmate."

"No, Brit. Not just anyone. You and I belong together."

"But you—" My bestie doesn't finish. She doesn't need to. I already bonded with someone. Became female. We had children. Who knows if I can bond again?

A sigh works its way up out of my gut. "Brit. I love you. Okay?" But I don't know if she can ever become a father. I pull my bestie close, shut my eyes, and wait till she's ready to lie down and wander off to sleep.

Chapter Thirty

Three weeks pass on Eilean nan Sìthean. Three weeks living with my bestie and her mom and their family. I'm home. I'm petite and blonde again. Brit thinks I'm wonderful. But the bits of my sanity—and the memories of the dead—still bounce around inside my skull. I can't focus on anything else.

How much of my time among Outsiders was fantasy? The loss of Courtenay—real or imagined—left me in need of healing. My body's no longer dying. I get that. But I see the darkness in my soul every time I look into Brit's eyes. Fear lives there as well. Fear that I'll shift away from her. Again.

We both knew I'd go back to An Gàrradh—the source of my watercolor landscapes. To find peace there. Or leave family and friends behind. Again. Perhaps never to return.

Brit—always a friend—urged me to face whatever might await me in the cherry grove. To make peace. Now, rather than live in such turmoil. Even if that meant she'd lose me.

Cold rain patters against my coat and runs down the slick fabric. On your Fahrenheit scale, the temperature sinks into the high forties. Clouds blanket the sky, though heather blooms in all its glory across the countryside. Yes—a gorgeous fall day on Eilean nan Sìthean. I breathe deep of the clean air, glad to be free of the asthma that plagued me while I was living as a human.

Brit wipes the hair from her face and grins at me. Yeah. We belong together. Now and forever. And, no, I haven't forgotten Courtenay. I will never forget him. Or Taylor or Remie. I pray that—somewhere in God's good creation—they're alive and well.

Kyrill's gone. The memories of Mamochka's death have faded. I'm content with my body now. Well almost. I don't think I'll have a problem when my hair turns ginger again, and I grow taller and more muscular. But fear still lurks in my dreams. What if this isn't the last stop? What if I slip into another reality and leave Brit alone?

So I lead my bestie down the cobblestone path to my watercolor memories. To the place where a blonde girl waited for someone who never came. To the granite boulder where I once sat. Till I slipped away. And abandoned my mother.

At the edge of An Gàrradh, Brit slips her hand out of mine and stops. "I'll wait here," she says. Her eyes convey only love. Yet she doesn't want to come with me to the place that's been at the center of my life. "Why?" Am I hurt? A little. Yet I trust her.

"I see things you don't, Annushka." Her fingertips brush down my arm. Annushka. Yeah, I guess she'd know that name if she saw me through my other Brits' eyes.

I walk on for a few paces, then look at her again. Brit will wait here, but what if I never return? What if I'm swept into the Outsiders' world? I don't want to be alone any more. So I walk back to my best friend. "I don't want to lose you," I say. I don't want to die alone.

Brit speaks words of encouragement to my soul. My ears hear nothing but the flapping of my coat in the wind. The girl pushes away my fears—and a few of the death memories that cling to my heart.

I inhale deep of the salt air and walk on. Down the cobblestone path. Into An Gàrradh. Beneath the sheltering arms of the cherry trees. To the granite boulder where I waited for so long.

I rest a bare hand on the frigid stone, remembering the happy times I spent with Courtenay in a similar place, thinking about my watercolor paintings, listening to the trees whisper to me as their branches rustled in the sea breeze.

The heart at my throat exudes a gentle warmth. It vibrates, almost like one of my children purring. Yeah. Like that.

"Anna," a voice says—a woman's tender welcoming call. The hair on the back of my neck stands on end. Muscles tense, then relax again. Memories flow as I turn—like the paint dripping down my watercolors—and I finally understand.

My mother gave herself to the sea after the Outsiders killed my father. As would any other bean-sìthe who lost her bondmate. Yet she stands before me now, clearly alive, water dripping from her hair and clothes. Terrified of losing her again, I rush to her open arms. How could I not? Minutes pass as she holds me. The rain slows and then stops. Reluctant sunbeams pierce the gray overcast. For a moment, the eternal sea breeze rests.

"Venora told me you'd returned."

My mother's voice calms my soul. I ease out of her grip and study the tender love on her face. It's been so long since we last spoke. She said that she loved me. She gave me her heart. Then she walked down the trail to Cladach Beag and out past the surf.

She told me to wait here in the grove. I did—for a short while—then ran after her, not understanding her sorrow, not knowing that my father had been killed by the Outsiders. A human patrol aircraft shot him while he sat in a boat just offshore, fishing.

Mother crossed the sandy beach, waded out to the remains of my father's boat, and, for what seemed like hours, wailed like a child while she held his dead body. Terrified, I fled back to the cherry grove and waited. The morning dawned before Peadar came and told me that I had to go stay with her family.

"I'm proud of what you did to the Outsider weapon."

I look up into my mother's face again. Yes. She still mourns the loss of her bondmate. Would she have given herself to the sea had she known it was a beginning rather than the end?

Memories of those long dead surge through me again. Yes, the Daoine-Sìth were powerful warriors. But it was the fear of their own cruelty—and what they were becoming—that led them to reject violence. They were more skilled at death than the humans who sought to kill them, but they laid down their weapons rather than exterminate their enemies.

She taps my heart with a fingertip. It flashes at her touch—I see its reflection in her eyes. "Yes. We make peace," she says. "But the Outsider weapons must be stopped. A thin rock wall stands between the Outsiders and death. If they release the Black Water, they will die. All of them."

I stare at the woman, mouth open. I'm nobody. Yeah, maybe Brit and I can stop a single drone. But even that almost killed me. Blinded her. I shake my head in helplessness. Me, the girl who's afraid of becoming a boy. Afraid of the normal adolescent transition from gold to red.

My mother smiles at me. "Why do you think I gave a precious heirloom to you rather than one of your sisters?"

I have no idea. Words fail me. So I just shake my head.

"You were our fifth child, so I already had quite a bit of experience nursing. But every time you began to feed, the heart vibrated in sync with your purring. Whenever you touched it, the metal glowed a light blue. Like áed burning deep inside."

"We bonded."

Memories of my early childhood reflect in her eyes. "No. The heart is—after all—just a piece of worked metal. You established the connection with it. Just as I did. Just as one of your own daughters shall."

My daughters? Mine? They're lost to me. Who knows if Brit and I will ever be able to have children? My lungs fill with the cold, damp air of Eilean nan Sìthean. I breathe it in and hold it against the ghosts that run through An Gàrradh. My first Brit. Her mother. Dylan. Jazmine. Dixie. Courtenay. The Zombie Apocalypse.

My mother wore the heart before me. She has to know. My eyes plead for understanding. "Mamochka. Màthair. Was any of it real?"

Her face turns serious. "You drowned," she says. As though that settles everything.

The world shifted, the bond was severed, and I lost Courtenay. Because I didn't have the heart with me? I shake my head. "I lost my bondmate."

Pain flashes from my mother's eyes. Muscles twitch. She pulls me tight. "I am so sorry, Anna." After a few minutes, she backs away and searches my face. "I did not know it possible to bond while in Am Beatha Eile."

The other life. My watercolor world. Fantasy. "Was Courtenay real?" Like she'd know my bondmate's name.

Her shoulders rise in a deep sigh. She looks away. Seconds pass as my heart thumps in my chest. My mother hugs me again before answering. "Real? Yes. Certainly. Did he exist? I don't think so. At least not in our world." Empathy flows from her eyes. "Did you have children?"

"Two." I take a deep breath to help fight off the pain. To avoid thinking about my daughters. But one of the ancient memories assures me they still exist. Somewhere in God's good creation. Maybe Courtenay does as well.

Minutes pass in silence while our eyes share our common sorrow. Finally, my mother takes my hand and leads me through the grove to An Oir—the Edge of the World. A cliff, actually, with the sea a hundred feet below us.

Trying to ignore l'appel du vide, I watch seagulls frolic in the updrafts. Here on Eilean nan Sìthean, I have someone to live for. I turn to my mother again. "How long was I away?"

She pulls me close once more before answering. "Almost a year."

A year ago. Then it began when my twin—the one I never had—returned my heart. Mamochka had already died. Kyrill been sent to prison. They were both only memories.

For a few minutes, we stand there—mother and daughter—enjoying the sea breeze and the salty mist. Then she turns to me. "I live down there now. Only Venora and Eachann spend much time on the island. If you need me, tell Eachann. He'll find me." She kisses me on the forehead. "For now, I must go." Three quick steps take her to the cliff. And over.

I rush to the edge, but the only thing in sight below me is the sea. And a giant white-tailed eagle, circling above the waves. I watch —not breathing—till she dives below the water's surface.

My hand rises to the heart at my throat. I stand there in the cold sea breeze. Till the rain starts again and the chill pushes through my coat. I walk back through An Gàrradh and along the cobblestone path to find Brit.

Chapter Thirty-One

The tall oaks rest their weary limbs after dancing in the heavy rain. High above, the afternoon sun peeks through dark gray clouds. Lightning flashes in the distance, but the storm has passed. I wipe the raindrops from my face, shake them from my coat, and ignore the voices in my head. Yes. My mother is gone.

I run a fingertip across the engraving on my heart. Nì Mi Sìth, it says—I'll make peace. Yet I have none. Not with the Outsiders. Not in my own heart. I glance back toward the Edge of the World. L'appel du vide beckons me, but giving myself to the sea would only mean becoming Daoine Mara. If I'm not already.

I gave Courtenay my heart—along with much of my self. That was supposed to heal her and let us both survive a shattered bond. Because we wouldn't remember each other. Or at least not feel the pain. Memories of the elders insisted that the heart itself could free us from our misery.

Fragments of life. Visions of death. Missing pieces. Myth. Fairy tale. And àeileanì—the metal from which the heart was forged. It bonds to a person more surely than two reds kissing. The heart found its way back to me—however improbable the journey. My memories—my self—are bleeding from the heart back into my soul.

My bestie stands in the cold, waiting for me. Relief shines from her eyes as I draw near. I slide my arms around the girl's waist and pull her close. "It's just you and me now, Brit."

She reaches a hand up to my face and wipes away my tears. Now as she did so long ago. Then she kisses my cheek. "So much sadness in your eyes, Annushka. I watched a beautiful bird land close by you. I hoped she would bring you peace."

Yeah. Peace. Not gonna happen. I hold Brit's hand tight as we walk back down the road toward the Aindréas homestead. Memories of Courtenay grow stronger with every step, the pain of losing my bondmate and our children greater than bouncing ever was. The heart grows warm against my chest.

People walking the other way eye us with concern. Two golds out in foul weather. Two frail girls. If we had enough ginger hair to have our braids cut, they wouldn't worry. People expect a red to be foolish—he's a boy.

Not far from halfway home, Brit stops and shakes her head. Then she turns and points back down the road toward Cladach Beag. "Another one's coming," she says. Frantic eyes study my face. My bestie's fear grows. Not for herself. For me. 'Cause I can't keep getting hit by lightning. Right now, dying wouldn't be so bad, actually. Except—yeah—I'd hurt Brit. And her mother. So I smile for her. "Maybe we can talk it into going back home."

This time, I find a place to sit. The mighty Daoine-Sìth warrior, about to defend her people from an Outsider weapon, and all she can think about is her lost bondmate. So I sit. And I wait. Till Brit stands behind me and puts her hands over my eyes.

A network of pulsing blue and gold filaments soars above the ocean, riding the updraft higher as it approaches the island. I reach out with care, hoping to learn something. With a gentle push, I press against some of the connections. Nothing I do alters the aircraft's course.

The drone talks to its handlers, sending video, selecting targets, reporting status. I press against their communications. Nothing. When I touch one of the shining nodes, energy flows into me—into Mamochka's heart. I draw in as much dealan as I can. A number of the filaments go dark. The aircraft turns. The configuration changes. The drone returns to its original course. Bombs ready.

Memories flood me. Daoine-Sìth. Human. Courtenay. Taylor. Remie. Of a sudden, dealan flows, taking all of my sorrow with it. Bright blue sparks carry my grief to the heavens—through the middle of the glowing network. They rain down on the cherry grove.

The filaments burst and scatter like fireworks in the night sky. Remains of the aircraft fall into the sea. My body sways, legs and arms going limp. I fall on my side, curl up in the heather, and puke till nothing remains. When I'm finished, and my breathing slows again, Brit helps me to my feet. "Something happened," she says, "We have to go back to An Oir."

Yeah. I felt it. The heart burns hot against my breast. Though I'm still here, something shifted. Not the Edge of the World, though. An Gàrradh—the cherry grove—where I waited for my mother. Where Courtenay and I spent so much of our time. Yes. There.

I raise a hand to check my burning fingers. A silver chain hangs from my clenched fist. When I pry open my hand, I find a heart. Like the one Mamochka gave me, but smaller. On one side is engraved Ceartas, Tròcair, Irioslachd—Justice, Mercy, Humility.

I close my eyes and think back to when I last spoke with Giselle. Is this hers? I remember most of my time with Courtenay, but some of the events at Dixie's place are fuzzy. I slide the heart into one of my pockets. Yeah, dude, Daoine-Sìth dresses have pockets. I nod at Brit and start the long walk back to An Gàrradh. "Can you see him from here?"

My bestie eyes me with overwhelming sorrow. "There are four," she says.

Is Brit afraid of losing me to Courtenay? The agony of my bond-mate's loss remains, like a dark void within. Yet I don't feel his presence or detect the faintest remnant of our bond. My bestie sees four, though, and one owns the heart I carry.

"Two are wee ones," she says. Yeah. Taylor and Remie. Her shoulders rise in a weary shrug. "One of the adults is Daoine-Sìth. I'm not sure about the other. Could be an Outsider."

I can be dense. I get that. Brit isn't sad for herself, but for me. Courtenay's dead.

My bestie slows as we approach An Gàrradh. Her eyes avoid mine. "Let me go ahead," she says. "Alone. You wait here."

I stop and draw in a deep breath. "I love you, Brit. Not sure what I'd do if I were alone right now. But I have to see his body."

My bestie's mouth works. She nods and looks away, but says nothing more.

I hear Taylor and Remie before I see them. Their frantic cries of, "Maman!" tear at my heart. When they're close enough, I scoop them up and hold them tight against my—my mother-sized boobs.

So, yeah. I can change shape. I must be Daoine Mara. And, by my babies' purring, the milk is real.

Courtenay and Giselle both lie next to the boulder where I waited for my mother. Where Dixie cut off my braid. Where my bondmate and I drank a toast to our marriage. Dead. Here.

I lost Courtenay long ago—at the Davydov estate—at Dixie's place—and again, when he walked out into the sea. The certainty of it, though a shock, only numbs the pain. One more fractured memory of death—I haven't the capacity to feel more sorrow. Not if I had Jazmine's drugs flowing through my veins.

The bodies aren't pretty. I refuse to think of what happened. Beyond the small round holes. And the dried blood. Not a comforting site. Brit helps me carry my bondmate's body to the moss bed he used for birthing our children. The plant wouldn't harm a living being, but it can dispose of a dead body in a few days. Once we arrange Courtenay, we cover him with flowers, mostly ròs a 'bhàis.

After we finish with Giselle's body, Brit and I sit for an hour or two. Together. Close. Till the setting sun and the chill sea breeze warn us of a cold night approaching. Till I can say goodbye to Courtenay. Forever this time. Though the empty spot in my soul remains.

After I stand, I help Brit to her feet. Both Taylor and Remie have burrowed under her coat, and probably her blouse as well. Like she was their mother instead of me. Fine. Let her carry them if she likes. It's a long walk home.

I pull Giselle's heart out of my pocket. In my time at Dixie's, the woman never mistreated me. Never lied to me, though she didn't speak to me much either. I didn't like her, but the words on her heart —Justice, Mercy, Humility—call on me to help return the heirloom to her family.

Six women survived the attack on Eilean nan Sìthean. They became the First Mothers of the Daoine-Sìth reborn. Long after the war, a seventh joined them. Though born on Eilean Dhiùra, Màili Camshròn was descended from the same bean-sìthe as the rest of the women. My gut says that she and Giselle were related. I know Màili well. Hope I don't hurt her.

Brit and I walk back home in silence. Just another day destroy-ing Outsider weapons, shifting family to an alternate reality, and burying a loved one. Yeah. Happens all the time. I grin at my bestie to ease the pain. "I love you," I whisper. 'Cause she doesn't want to hear me say it aloud.

Taylor peeks out from the middle of Brit's cloak. "Papa," she says and taps on my bestie's chest. Somewhere underneath the coat, Remie squeaks agreement. Daoine-Sìth children tend to be mother's girls and then father's boys. Yeah, they probably miss Courtenay. But Brit's here.

My bestie finally makes eye contact again. Love, sorrow, and joy wrestle there. Not a word, though. She just nods agreement. That I love her? Or that she'll be Papa for them? I stop and wait. What else can I do? I take several deep breaths, hoping to slow my crazy heart. Minutes pass before Brit meets my eyes again. "I want this," she says. "Us. A family." The sorrow in her eyes grows.

Yeah. Sadness on her face. 'Cause we're not two reds. I already bonded. Brit can't. She may never be able to. And our people may not understand.

But the Daoine-Sìth elders from my dead memories lived closer to a merciful God than we do. Justice, Mercy, Humility—Peace—they pursued such things. Those incapable of a physical bond could still establish a covenant—a lifelong commitment to one another. And so shall we. Soon.

I take Brit's hand in mine. With my other, I brush a fingertip across the heart at my throat. It glows in response. Nì Mi Sìth. We'll make peace. With the Outsiders. With the Daoine-Sìth. With ourselves.

The End

If you enjoyed this story, please leave a review.

Dedication

To my father and mother,
who first encouraged
curiosity, imagination,
and reading,
and who never treated
my physical differences
as something shameful.

As a small and frail child,
one with a cute pixie face,
I imagined that
I might be a changeling.

Indeed,
our Kirkpatrick ancestors
were thought to be fae.

Outsider
A Forbidden Island Short Story

In the closing hours of World War II, an experimental weapon meant for London struck Eilean nan Sìthean, a remote Scottish island. Within forty-eight hours, all of the men there died. Six months later, the few women who survived gave birth to the children of the plague —the Fair Folk of Scottish mythology reborn. Nearly seventy years later, a young gold named Màiri discovers an Outsider washed ashore—the first human she's ever seen. Saving his life would mean spending the rest of her days with a stranger, the sworn enemy of her people. But she cannot let him die alone.

Confessions of a Teenage Hermaphrodite

From the heart of an intersex teen, one who must ultimately choose male or female—family or true love—comes the story of a deeply emotional and perilous journey home. This is a young adult novel unlike any other—an authentic portrayal of the issues faced by a child growing up with a sexually ambiguous body.

Jameson can be like other boys after minor surgery and a few years on testosterone Well, at least that's what his parents always say. But Jamie sees an elfin princess in the mirror, and male hormones would only ruin her pretty face. For him to become the man his parents expect, Jameson must leave behind the hopes and dreams of a little girl. But what is so wrong with Jamie's dreams that they can't be her life?

A Proper Young Lady

A woman with the complete form of Androgen Insensitivity Syndrome might never discover that she has testes in her abdomen rather than ovaries and uterus. Danièle knows, and she grieves that she can never have her own children. She has a partial form of AIS that left her with ambiguous genitals, a steady stream of doctors and psychologists, and parents determined to see her happy as a girl.

After Danièle's best friend and childhood crush agrees to act as a surrogate for her, Danièle learns that the clinic can extract sperm from her own gonadal biopsies, so she becomes the biological father of Melanie's baby herself.

Ethan adores the graceful young woman named Danièle, while Melanie imagines a life with the father of her children. Danièle? She's happy with her intersex body—somewhere between princess and little boy. But in a black and white world, she must choose— once and for all—who she will be. And whom she will love.